"Well, well, look what we got here, Lem," Joe said. "Why didn't you tell us last night he was your kid, Mister?"

"He's not my kid."

"Then what's he doin' with you?"

"We're just going to get something to eat."

"What's goin' on, Mister?" Lem asked. "Are you with this kid? You lookin' for Dead Horse Canyon, too?"

"Right now," Clint said, "we're just looking for something to eat, so step aside and let us pass."

"Naw, naw," Joe said, "wait a minute. This kid was asking a lot of questions last night, and then you came in and started asking—"

"You've got it wrong, friend," Clint said. "You were the one asking me the questions, and I wasn't answering them, remember?"

"Yeah, I do remember . . ."

"So if I wasn't answering your questions last night," Clint continued, "what makes you think I'll answer them now?"

Clint started forward but Joe held his left hand out, his right hovering just above his gun.

"You just ain't very friendly, are you, friend?"

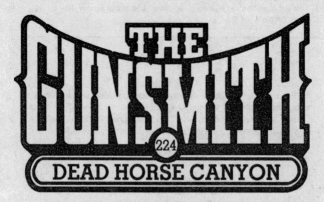

THE GUNSMITH

224

DEAD HORSE CANYON

J. R. ROBERTS

JOVE BOOKS, NEW YORK

DEAD HORSE CANYON

A Jove Book / published by arrangement with
the author

PRINTING HISTORY
Jove edition / August 2000

All rights reserved.
Copyright © 2000 by Robert J. Randisi.
This book may not be reproduced in whole or part,
by mimeograph or any other means, without permission.
For information address: The Berkley Publishing Group,
a division of Penguin Putnam Inc.,
375 Hudson Street, New York, New York 10014.

The Penguin Putnam Inc. World Wide Web site address is
http://www.penguinputnam.com

ISBN: 0-515-12891-0

A JOVE BOOK®
Jove Books are published by The Berkley Publishing Group,
a division of Penguin Putnam Inc.,
375 Hudson Street, New York, New York 10014.
JOVE and the "J" design
are trademarks belonging to Penguin Putnam Inc.

PRINTED IN THE UNITED STATES OF AMERICA

10 9 8 7 6 5 4 3 2 1

ONE

Clint Adams was extremely pleased with the performance of his new horse, Eclipse. The animal was a Darley Arabian Thoroughbred brought to this country from Europe by P. T. Barnum and presented to Clint as a gift for saving the lives of the old showman and his young wife, Nancy. He was a descendant of the great stallion Eclipse but that was only one reason Clint had given his new horse the same name. The other reason was that the animal was as black as night everywhere except right between his eyes, where there was a white crescent, like the sliver of light that peeks out from behind an eclipse.

It had been a month since Clint had returned to the West from New York with Eclipse. He had taken the horse directly to Labyrinth, Texas, to seek the approval of two of his closest friends.

Rick Hartman had examined the animal completely and pronounced him fit and magnificently put together.

"The proof, however," Hartman had said, "will be found on the trail."

After that Clint took Eclipse to the nearby ranch where his big black gelding, Duke, who he had ridden for years,

1

had been put out to pasture. He turned Eclipse out into the same pasture and watched the two horses as they got acquainted.

Eclipse did not have Duke's sheer size and mass, but Duke did not have the conformation that the Darley Arabian had. The two animals ignored each other for a while and then the younger colt—a three-year-old—had gone over to the older gelding, who was easily three times the age of the other, and more. Duke turned and walked away from the younger horse, but did not immediately run him off.

That was approval enough for Clint.

He had been riding the colt for a month now, and the animal had done everything asked of him and more. He had demonstrated not only speed, but stamina as well, which were the two characteristics Clint had been looking for in a new horse during the months since Duke had been turned out.

And so it was on their one-month anniversary as horse and rider that Clint and Eclipse rode into the town of Broken Branch, Colorado, simply because it was there. Clint wanted a drink, wanted to give Eclipse some feed and a rubdown. The animal had been performing well, but so too had Clint been taking very good care of him.

Broken Branch was a small town with the look of one that would not soon become any larger. It had a telegraph, though, and a livery, a saloon, a hotel and a sheriff's office, as well as a bank. It had everything it needed and, as Clint rode down the main street at midday, there were plenty of people coming and going.

Clint reached the livery and dismounted.

"Nice looking animal," the liveryman said. He'd been hearing that for a month. He'd heard it for many years while riding Duke, but always with some awe due to

Duke's sheer size. The compliments he received about Eclipse had more to do with admiration than awe.

"If you don't mind," Clint said, "I'd like to rub him down and feed him myself."

"Sure thing," the liveryman said. "I don't mind. Less work for me. New to you, is he?"

"It shows?"

"I've seen lots of men and horses in my sixty-three years, Mister," the man said, "and you and this one got that look."

"What look?"

"The still getting to know each other look."

The man showed Clint to a stall in the stable and he proceeded to unsaddle Eclipse, rub him down well and then feed him. That done, he grabbed his saddlebags and rifle and went off to see who he could find to do the same things for him—give him a place to stay and rest, and something to eat.

Clint got a room at the nearby Kelton Hotel but stayed in his room just long enough to drop off his gear and test the bed. The bed was fine, so the next thing on his agenda was a meal and a drink.

As he left the hotel he saw a man with a badge pushing a prisoner ahead of him. They were crossing the street to get to the sheriff's office on the other side. The sheriff was a big, beefy man in his forties who probably could have pushed the prisoner with his belly just as easily as with his hands.

A lawman walking a prisoner to jail was not unusual, but this case was a little different in that the prisoner looked to be all of fourteen or fifteen years old, and skinny as a rail.

It looked as if the sheriff could have picked the boy up and snapped him like a twig. Instead, he kept on shoving him even though the boy did not seem to be dragging his feet. In fact, the lad seemed to be walking with all the dignity he could muster. He wasn't hanging his head, and his shoulders were not slumped. Clint stopped and watched as the odd twosome reached the jail and entered, and then continued on in his quest for something to eat and drink. However, he wasn't quite able to totally push the scene he'd just witnessed from his mind.

TWO

Clint went past the saloon first, but decided to eat before he stopped in for a drink. There were a couple of men just inside the batwing doors, though, and he could hear their conversation as he went past.

". . . troublemaking kid," one of them was saying. "Why didn't you put a bullet in him, Lem?"

"How would it look for me to shoot a kid, you idiot," the other man said. "He ain't gonna be no trouble in jail. Let's get back to our drinks."

"I still think you shoulda . . ." the other man was saying as they faded out of earshot.

Clint kept walking, but was thinking about the boy. What kind of trouble could he have started with two hardcases like that? Did he even have a gun? He didn't recall seeing the sheriff carrying a gun, but he might have had it tucked into his belt. He certainly had enough of a belly to hide a gun.

Despite the fact that he was curious, Clint decided to mind his own business. A meal and a drink, and a good night's sleep, that was all he wanted from the town of Broken Branch.

He kept walking until he encountered a small café and

went inside. It was pretty empty, since it was past lunch time, so he was able to be seated and served very quickly. He ordered a steak, hoping they wouldn't overcook it, and was pleasantly surprised when it arrived still oozing blood. It was also surrounded by carrots and potatoes that were done just right. Heartened, he decided to try the coffee as well, but quickly learned that was a mistake. It was very weak, and he did not risk a second sip, preferring instead to wash his meal down with water.

He found himself thinking about the trouble with the young boy all through the meal and was still mulling it over as he left. He headed back to the saloon where he'd heard the two men talking, hoping that they'd still be there. Maybe he'd be able to overhear something else.

He entered the Broken Branch Saloon and walked directly to the bar. Three of the tables in the place were occupied, two of them by two men sitting together. At the third table sat a lone man nursing a beer.

"Help ya?"

He turned to see the bartender looking up at him. He was looking up because he seemed to be about five foot two. Any shorter and he might not have been able to see over the bar.

"Beer," he said.

"Comin' up."

The bartender brought him his beer and walked off, leaving him alone, which suited him. He wanted to see if he could hear anything from the tables that would tell him which pair of men he'd overheard at the door. He kept his back to the room, though, to keep anyone from suspecting that he was trying to eavesdrop.

As it turned out he wasn't able to hear much. Two of the men did not seem to be talking, while the other two were keeping their voices down.

Then he got lucky.

From the table a man rose and walked to the bar to get himself and his friend another beer. While at the bar he called out to his partner.

"Shoulda shot him, Lem, I'm tellin' ya."

"Keep yer trap shut, Joe," Lem said back to him. "Ain't nobody else's business what went on, or why."

"The bartender saw it," Joe said, "didn't ya, barkeep?"

"The boy was lookin' for trouble," the bartender said, setting two more beers on the bar for them.

"See?" Joe said. "He was askin' for it."

Suddenly, Joe looked at Clint, who made the mistake of turning his head at that moment.

"Whataya think, Mister?"

"About what?"

"About a kid with a gun lookin' fer trouble."

"I wasn't here."

"I'm tellin' ya," Joe said. "He comes in here askin' questions, lookin' fer trouble, and then came over to me and my friend."

"Asking questions is looking for trouble?" Clint asked. "I didn't know that."

"Well, it depends on what yer askin' about," Joe said.

"Joe," Lem called, "bring the beer over here and shut up."

"I just wanted to get this fella's opinion, is all," Joe groused.

"He don't care to hear it," Lem said, "and neither do I."

"That right, friend?" Joe asked. "You don't care to hear about it, and gimme your opinion?"

Clint looked at the man. He was in his twenties— maybe ten years older than the boy. His trail clothes were worn, like he'd been riding for a while. Then he turned and looked at the man who was still seated. He was in his thirties, but wearing the same kind of worn trail clothes.

"I apologize for my partner, Mister," Lem said. "He don't mean nothin', he's just an idiot."

"Don't be tellin' nobody I'm an idiot, Lem," the man called Joe complained.

"Then bring those beers over here and shut the hell up!"

Grumbling, Joe finally did as his friend said and went back to the table.

Clint waved the bartender over and asked for another beer. When he brought the second mug he spoke to the man.

"What was that about?" he asked.

"Aw, some kid came in and tried to start trouble."

"By asking questions?"

"Nobody likes some wet behind the ears kid comin' in and askin' a buncha questions," the bartender said.

"What about me?" Clint asked. "I'm not wet behind the ears. Mind if I ask a question?"

The little bartender backed up a step, but said, "Uh, sure, Mister, go ahead and ask."

"What was the boy asking about?"

"He wanted to know the whereabouts of a place called, um, Wild Horse Canyon, I think."

Clint paused a moment, then asked the man, "Could it have been Dead Horse Canyon?"

"Yeah, that was it," the bartender said. "Dead Horse Canyon. He wanted to know if nobody knew where it was."

Clint fell silent.

"You know somethin' about it, Mister?"

Clint looked him in the eye and said, "Didn't anybody

ever tell you nobody likes being asked questions?"

"But you said—" the bartender started, then stopped, turned and walked away from Clint as if he were walking on eggshells.

THREE

Clint had indeed heard of Dead Horse Canyon. He wondered why a boy of fourteen or fifteen would be looking for it? He wondered why he should even care? He'd had his meal and his drink, and all he needed now was a good night's sleep before he moved on. Her didn't need to get involved with some boy who was looking for a fabled outlaw hideout that most people were convinced didn't exist.

The only problem with that was Clint Adams knew that it *did* exist. He'd never been there, but he had it on pretty good authority that it was real, and he had some idea of where to find it.

Left alone the boy would probably go on searching and never find it. He'd probably quit, depending on what was driving him. But if he didn't quit, and he managed to find it . . . then what?

Well, the answer to that question was fairly obvious—he'd end up getting himself killed.

Clint finally decided he'd try to talk to the boy, just to satisfy his curiosity. He crossed the street and walked to the sheriff's office. As he entered the beefy lawman looked up from his desk.

"Help ya?" the man asked.

"I understand you have a boy in one of your cells."

"I got a prisoner," the sheriff said. "You a lawman?"

"No."

"His father?"

"No."

"What's your interest?"

"I was just wondering what you arrested him for," Clint said.

"He was disturbin' the peace in the saloon."

"Is that all?"

"I'm just keepin' him overnight until he cools off."

"Well, how about letting him out in my custody?"

"Do you know this boy?"

"Never saw him before I saw you pushing him across the street," Clint said.

"Then what's your interest?"

"I just don't like seeing a young boy spend the night in jail."

"Well," the lawman said, rubbing his jaw, "I guess I could let him out, but there's a fine . . ."

Clint took some money out and laid it on the desk.

"I think this would cover his fine."

"Yep," the sheriff said, sweeping the money off the desktop and into a drawer with one swift move, "that'll do 'er." He stood up and grabbed the cell keys from a peg on the wall. "I'll get him for ya, but I gotta warn ya, he's ornery as hell."

"Thanks for the warning."

The sheriff went into the back and returned with the boy, pushing him ahead of him. Up close the young man looked more like sixteen. He had long, shaggy hair that hid his eyes, and no stubble whatsoever on his chin. He was not tall, and he was thin, all elbows and knees, it looked like.

"What's his name?" Clint asked.

"Beats me," the sheriff said. "I couldn't get that out of him." The sheriff nudged the boy hard in the back, hard enough to propel him a step or two forward.

"You ought to thank this man, kid," the lawman said. "He paid your fine. You're in his custody until tomorrow."

The boy didn't say anything, but he did brush the hair out of his eyes to take a look at Clint.

"Okay, thanks, Sheriff," Clint said. "I'll take it from here. Come on, son. Let's get you out of here."

Clint walked to the door, turned and saw that the boy hadn't moved.

"You coming?" he asked. "Or staying in jail?"

The boy looked behind him at the sheriff, then followed Clint, who opened the door and let the boy out first.

Outside, the boy stopped dead in his tracks.

"Am I going to have to tug you around?" Clint asked.

"You ain't after no funny stuff, are you?" the boy asked.

"What?"

"You know what I mean," the boy said. "I don't do that stuff."

Clint studied the boy for a few moments, and then said, "Don't flatter yourself, son. You're not that pretty. You hungry?"

"I could eat."

"Yeah, well, I ate already, but I could do with a piece of pie and some coffee. Come on, then," Clint said. "I'll feed you and then maybe you'll figure I've at least earned the right to hear your name."

FOUR

"Todd," the boy said, after he'd put away enough food for two grown men.

"Todd what?"

He didn't answer.

"I guess that's all I get for now, huh?"

"Why'd you get me out of jail?" Todd asked.

"I saw the sheriff pushing you across the street," Clint said. "I just didn't like the way it looked. I also went into the saloon. They told me you caused a lot of trouble in there."

"I was only asking some questions."

"I heard about that, too."

"Nobody wants to tell me where Dead Horse Canyon is."

"Not many men know," Clint said. "In fact, not many men believe it really exists."

"I believe it does."

"And why do you want to go there?"

Todd mulled the question over, and then said, "That's my business."

"You're right, it is," Clint said, "but if I'm going to be of any help to you I'll have to make it my business."

15

"I didn't ask you for no help."

"That's right, you didn't," Clint said. "I can always take you back to the jail and leave you there overnight."

"No, don't do that."

"Where did you sleep last night?"

"On the trail."

"You just got to town today?"

"That's right."

"So did I. Where did you plan on sleeping tonight?"

"In the livery. I already got the man to agree to let me sleep in the hayloft," Todd said.

"That was good thinking."

"It wasn't hard," the boy said. "I ain't got that much money."

"How old are you?"

He didn't answer.

"Surely I earned that much by feeding you and getting you out of jail," Clint said, "don't you think?"

"Sixteen."

"And how long have to been looking for Dead Horse Canyon?"

"A long time."

"Since when?"

"Since my ma died."

"I'm sorry," Clint said. "When was that?"

"Six months ago."

"Where?"

"Kentucky."

"That where you're from?"

Todd seemed to be loosening up some, as he nodded. At least they were getting *somewhere*.

"Is this something your ma wanted you to do, Todd?"

"No," he said, "she don't . . . didn't . . . want me to go nowhere near Dead Horse Canyon."

"Then why do you want to?"

Todd hesitated, then said, "I got to, that's all."

"I see," Clint said, even though he didn't, really. "Have you had enough to eat yet?"

"Yeah, I have," Todd said.

"When was the last time you ate?"

"I eat," the boy said, "just not like this. I can't afford it."

"How do you make money?"

"I do some odd jobs when I run out, then I get movin' again."

"Why are you in Colorado?"

"I heard Dead Horse Canyon was here."

"Where did you hear that?"

"My ma said it once."

"And how did she know?"

"I'm tired," Todd said. "I can't answer no more questions tonight."

"Okay," Clint said. "Let's go, I'll walk you over to the livery so you can get some sleep."

"Okay."

On the street Clint said, "You don't have to answer any more of my questions, if you don't want to."

"You gonna send me back to jail?"

"Nope," Clint said, "I'm going to let you get a good night's sleep and then send you on your way."

"I can leave town?"

"Yes, you can," Clint said. "In fact, I think it would be a fine idea."

"And no more questions?"

"I promise," Clint said, "that I won't ask anymore questions . . . unless you ask me for help."

"Well, I ain't—"

"That's fine," Clint said. "If you don't need my help, that's fine. Every man's got things he's got to do."

"That's right."

When they reached the livery the liveryman spotted Clint and came out.

"You gonna bed your own horse down, Mr. Adams, or you want me to do it?" he asked.

"You can do it," Clint said. "I just wanted to get him rubbed down and fed real quick this afternoon."

"You still sleepin' here?" the man asked Todd.

"If it's okay with you."

"Fine," the man said, "but you gotta sweep up before you turn in."

"I'll do it."

The man waved and went inside.

"Well," Clint said, "good luck."

The boy shuffled his feet, then said, "Thanks for getting me out of jail, and for the food."

"Sure . . . and do yourself a favor."

"What?"

"Don't ask anybody anymore questions in this town."

"Okay."

Clint waved, waited for the boy to go inside, and then walked away.

Inside the livery the boy asked the liveryman, "Hey, do you know who that feller was?"

"You mean you don't?"

"No."

"That there was Clint Adams, boy," the man said. "The Gunsmith."

Todd's eyes went wide as he recognized the name.

"If he's befriendin' you for any reason you're a lucky lad."

Sure, Todd thought, except he had just finished telling the Gunsmith he didn't want his help!

FIVE

When Clint came down to the hotel lobby the next morning, he wasn't surprised to find Todd waiting for him. If the boy had any brains at all he would have asked the liveryman who Clint was. When he found out the answer, he would have to have been totally brainless not to come to the hotel.

"Good morning, Todd."

"Can we talk some more?"

"Sure," Clint said. "How about over breakfast?"

"Okay."

Clint took Todd into the hotel dining room. When the waiter came Clint deliberately ordered a big breakfast and Todd simply told the waiter that he would have the same.

"What did you want to talk to me about?"

"Yesterday, when I said I didn't want your help? I didn't know who you were, then."

"Why is that important?"

"It just is."

"It wasn't yesterday," Clint said. "You didn't even bother asking me who I was yesterday."

"Well . . ."

"You were too busy being tough."

Todd didn't speak.

"So now you want my help?"

"Yes."

"To do what?"

"To find Dead Horse Canyon."

"And then what?"

Todd sat up straighter and said, "And then I want to kill everyone in it."

The breakfast came quickly and they tucked into it. It gave Clint enough time to think. The only motivation the boy could have for wanting to kill everyone they found in Dead Horse Canyon was revenge.

"You're going to have to tell me a lot more than you've been telling, Todd, before I'll agree to help you."

"I'll tell you anything you want to know," the boy said, around a mouthful of food.

"Now that you know who I am?"

"Right."

"Why?"

"Because with your help," he said, "I know I can do what I got to do."

"All right, Todd," Clint said. "Suppose we finish our breakfast first, and then you tell me why you want to kill everyone in Dead Horse Canyon. Deal?"

Todd nodded and said, "Deal."

"They killed my ma," Todd said, after they had finished eating.

"Who did?"

"The men who hide out in Dead Horse Canyon."

"And you know who they are?"

"I know one of 'em," he said. "That's all I got to know."

"Okay," Clint said, "then who is the one you know?"

Todd firmed his chin and said, "My pa."

"Let me get this straight," Clint said. "Your pa rides with the gang that hides out in Dead Horse Canyon."

"That's right."

"And how did he kill your ma?"

"He broke her heart."

"Todd," Clint said, "as painful as it may be, people don't die of a broken heart."

"She did," the boy insisted. "He shamed her."

"How?"

"He and his men robbed the whole town," Todd said. "And then he left us there to live with that."

"And you want to kill him for that?"

"Yes."

"How old were you when it happened?"

"Twelve when it happened," the boy said, "and fifteen when she died."

"That's three years of hate, boy," Clint said. "That's an awful lot."

"I got a right."

"Yeah, I guess you do, the way you look at it."

"There's only one way to look at it, Mr. Adams."

"You're going to have to call me Clint, if we're going to get along."

"Okay . . . Clint. Will you help me?"

"I'll help you find Dead Horse Canyon," Clint said, "only because I don't want you getting yourself killed doing it."

"And then you'll help me kill everyone there?"

"And then we'll see what happens when we get there," Clint said. "I'm not making any promises to kill anyone right now."

"Well . . ." Todd said, as if thinking it over. "I guess that's a start."

"Do you even have a gun?"

"I got an old Henry rifle that used to belong to my pa," Todd said. "That's all he left me. Before he left he tol' me to make sure I learned how to use it."

"And did you?"

"I sure did," Todd said, "and when I find him I'm gonna use it on him!"

SIX

Clint and Todd walked to the livery where the boy showed Clint both his rifle and his horse. Each had seen better days, but the rifle was much more functional than the horse was. Besides, Clint knew the boy would never give up the rifle, not with the plans he had for it.

"But you do need a new horse," Clint said. "This one will never keep up with mine."

"I can't afford a horse," Todd said.

"Well, I'll buy you a new one rather than let you ride this one into the ground," Clint said.

They got together with the liveryman, who took them to a corral out back where Clint picked out a five-year-old Mustang for Todd. The animal was fit, and was not very large. It would not be difficult for the boy to control.

"Will it keep up with yours?" Todd asked.

"We won't be racing," Clint said, "so it'll keep up."

"When can we leave?" Todd asked.

"In the morning. We'll have to get outfitted with some supplies, and you could use some new clothes."

"I can't pay you back the money you're spending, Clint," Todd said.

"Maybe you can."

"How?"

"We'll talk about that later," Clint said. "Maybe all I'll want in return is a favor. You'd be able to do that, wouldn't you?"

Carefully, Todd said, "I guess that would depend on what the favor was."

Clint smiled and said, "Smart kid."

They left the livery and went back to town. Clint told Todd that he'd better start carrying the rifle with him wherever he went.

"You'll never know when you'll need it."

"Good idea."

"Have you ever shot anyone, Todd?"

The boy hesitated, then said, "No."

"Ever shot anything?"

"Well, sure," Todd said. "I been hunting."

"What was the first thing you ever shot?"

"A deer."

"How did you feel afterwards?"

"Sick."

"Well, magnify that ten times and that's how you'll feel the first time you kill a man."

"I got over it," Todd said. "Besides, I only intend to kill somebody who deserves to die—my pa and his men."

"Tell me more about your pa and this gang," Clint said. "Is your pa the gang's leader?"

"No, he's second," Todd said. "The gang is led by a man named Atkins."

"Trace Atkins?" Clint asked.

"That's right," Todd said, impressed. "You know him?"

"I know his reputation," Clint said. "If I remember correctly there's about six men in the Atkins gang."

"That's right."

"Which one is your father?"

Suddenly, Todd realized that once he told Clint his father's name, he'd be telling him his own as well.

"You have the same last name?" Clint asked, realizing what was going through the boy's head at that moment.

"Yes."

"And you're ashamed of it?"

"Yes."

"Well," Clint said, "I guess I can let you keep it to yourself a little bit longer, then . . . just until you're ready to tell me on your own."

"Okay," Todd said. After a moment he added, "Thanks."

SEVEN

They went to the general store after that to arrange for some supplies—beef jerky, some canned goods, and coffee, mostly—and also for some clothes for Todd. When they were done he was wearing a new shirt and a new pair of Levis—clothes that *fit*, for a change—and also had another shirt under his arm. Clint gave Todd the sack of supplies to take to the livery with him.

"Since you're sleeping there," he said, "you might as well saddle the horses in the morning."

"Why me?"

"Because," Clint said, "if we're going to be riding together we're going to have to split up the chores."

"What're you gonna do?"

"Me?" Clint said. "I'm the money man."

After they stored the supplies and extra shirt at the livery, Clint told Todd to grab his rifle and they went around behind the livery.

"I want to see how well you can shoot," Clint said.

"Whataya want me to shoot at?"

"Something away from town, just in case."

"Don't worry," the boy said. "I can hit what I aim at."

27

"Okay," Clint said. "That tree, the big one with the branches sticking out like two arms? See it?"

The boy looked at him.

"That's better'n a hundred yards."

"Good," Clint said, "you can see it. Now hit it."

The boy didn't look confident, but he raised the rifle to his shoulder, aimed and fired. Clint could see that he missed.

"I'll go see if I hit it," Todd said.

"Never mind," Clint said. "If you had hit it, you'd know."

The boy lowered the rifle.

"Well, it's a hundred yards."

"Or more."

"And it's an old rifle."

"It's your gun," Clint said. "The one you want to use."

"I'll be closer."

"You should be able to hit that tree."

"Let me see you hit it."

"Give me your rifle."

Todd handed it over.

"Where do you want me to hit it?"

"Dead center."

"That's easy."

"Yea, lemme see—"

Clint raised the rifle and fired. They both saw the bullet kick some bark off the tree dead center.

Todd looked at Clint, wide-eyed.

"You didn't even aim."

"You don't aim a weapon, son," Clint said. "You point with it. You should be able to hit anything you can see, and point at."

"H-hit the branch on the right."

Clint raised the rifle and sheered the branch off the tree by hitting it right where it joined the trunk.

"And the left," he said, and fired again. The left branch flew off. He lowered the rifle and handed it back to Todd. "What can you hit?"

"Put a bottle or somethin' on that big white rock."

"That's about forty yards," Clint said. "You *can* do that?"

"Yes, sir."

Clint went into the livery, looked around and found a couple of empty whiskey bottles. The veins in the liveryman's nose had led him to believe he might.

He came out, walked to the rock and put one bottle on it, then came back to stand beside Todd.

"Okay," he said, "hit it."

Todd raised the rifle, aimed and fired, shattering the bottle.

"Okay," Clint said, "but do it faster this time. Don't aim, just point."

"I got to aim."

"No," Clint said, "you don't. Point!"

He walked back to the rock and placed the second bottle on it, then returned to stand by the boy.

"Do it."

The boy looked dubious, but he tensed and made ready to raise the rifle.

"Stop!"

Todd looked startled and glared at Clint.

"You tryin' to make me miss?"

"I'm trying to make sure you hit it," Clint said. "Relax, don't tense up, and *don't* hold your breath before you fire. You would have missed for sure."

Todd lowered the rifle, made an effort to relax himself, then raised the rifle and fired in one motion. He missed the bottle, but a split second later it shattered as Clint drew and fired.

"Wow!" Todd said. He looked at Clint. "Can you teach me to shoot like that?"

"It takes a lot of practice," Clint said. He ejected the spent shell, inserted a fresh round and holstered the gun. "Until it becomes second nature, and then no amount of practice will make you better."

"Can you teach me with a handgun?"

"Let's work on the rifle first," Clint said, "and then maybe we'll talk about a handgun. Wait here while I find a few more bottles . . ."

EIGHT

After shooting for another half hour Clint figured Todd was as good as he was going to get that day.

"Are you hungry?"

"Yes," Todd said.

"Come on, we'll get something to eat."

"Will you buy me a pistol?" Todd asked as they walked back to the center of town.

"I've been buying you what you need, Todd," Clint said. "That's something you want. You'll have to earn the money for that and buy it yourself."

"I will," Todd said. "I will earn it."

"Besides," Clint said, "from what you tell me you won't need a handgun to do what you want to do. You're going to use the rifle to kill your father, right?"

"That's right."

"And what will you do after that?"

"What do you mean?"

"I mean after he's dead, where will you go? Where will you live? Will you go back home?"

"No," Todd said, "that's not home to me anymore. I can't go back there."

"Then where?"

"I don't know."

"Well," Clint said, "when you do know, and when you get there, you can get a job and buy yourself a gun."

As they got to the center of town Clint was wondering if they should eat in the hotel, the café or find someplace else when he saw two men coming out of the saloon. They were the same two men he'd talked to the night before, Lem and Joe.

"Uh-oh," he said.

"What?"

"Friends of yours."

Todd looked and recognized the two men.

"They got real mad when I asked about Dead Horse Canyon," he said. "I think if I'd had a gun with me they would have killed me. They're the ones who got me arrested."

"I know," Clint said. "I met them last night."

"I have a gun with me now," Todd said. "What do we do if they—"

"Just relax," Clint said, as the two men spotted them. "Let me do the talking."

"All right."

They kept walking and stopped only when the two men barred the way.

"Well, well, look what we got here, Lem," Joe said. "Why didn't you tell us last night he was your kid, Mister?"

"He's not my kid."

"Then what's he doin' with you?"

"We're just going to get something to eat."

"What's goin' on, Mister?" Lem asked. "Are you with this kid? You lookin' for Dead Horse Canyon, too?"

"Right now," Clint said, "we're just looking for something to eat, so step aside and let us pass."

"Naw, naw," Joe said, "wait a minute. This kid was

asking a lot of questions last night, and then you came in and started asking—"

"You've got it wrong, friend," Clint said. "You were the one asking me the questions, and I wasn't answering them, remember?"

"Yeah, I do remember . . ."

"So if I wasn't answering your questions last night," Clint continued, "what makes you think I'll answer them now?"

Clint started forward but Joe held his left hand out, his right hovering just above his gun.

"You just ain't very friendly, are you, friend?"

"I told you," Clint said, "I'm not looking for a friend, just for something to eat."

"Mister," Todd said, "you better take your hand away from your gun."

"Now the little twerp is threatening me?" Joe asked. "And he's got a gun now? You threatenin' me, kid?"

"I ain't threatenin' you," Todd said, "just warnin' you. You don't know who you're dealin' with here."

"Todd—" Clint said. He knew what the boy was about to do, and it wasn't necessarily going to have the result that Todd expected. Knowing who he was might make these men want to go for their guns even more, instead of dissuading them. It depended on how badly they wanted their own reputations enhanced.

"Why don't you tell us, kid?" Joe asked. "Who are we dealin' with here?"

"This here's Clint Adams," Todd said.

Joe and Lem exchanged a glance and then Joe laughed and said, "You expect us to believe this is the Gunsmith?"

"He *is* the Gunsmith," Todd said.

"If he's the Gunsmith," Joe asked, "what's he doin' with you?"

"He's helpin' me," Todd said.

"Do what?" Lem asked. "Find Dead Horse Canyon?" Lem looked at Clint. "What about it, Mister? You really Clint Adams?"

"I'm really hungry," Clint said, "and that's all I'm telling you, right now. Anything else you're going to have to find out for yourself."

The two men exchanged another glance, unsure now of what they wanted to do. They wished they had time to talk it over.

"You don't want to keep your hand near your gun, Mister," Todd warned Joe.

Joe pulled his hand away from his weapon as if he'd been scalded, then immediately became angry with himself that he'd done it.

"Time to step aside, boys," Clint said. "I'm getting hungrier by the minute."

Joe looked at Lem and said, "Let the man pass, Joe."

Lem stepped to one side, and Joe to the other, to allow both Clint and Todd to go by.

"You think he really is the Gunsmith?" Joe asked.

"I think we can probably find out," Lem said. "Come on."

NINE

They chose to eat in the café again, and Todd could hardly contain his excitement until they were seated.

"Did you see that?" he asked.

"What?"

"They backed down, just because of who you are!" the boy said excitedly.

"They backed down," Clint said, "because they weren't sure of who I was. You could have been lying."

"They believed me!"

"They're going to check it out."

"How? With who?"

"With the sheriff."

"Does he know who you are?"

"No," Clint said, after a moment. He had to think back to recall whether or not he'd introduced himself to the lawman.

"Then the only way they can check it out," Todd said, "is to try you, and they won't do that."

"Oh? Why not?"

"Because they're scared!" The boy was bouncing up and down in his chair. "It must be great to be you!"

"Why?"

"Because people are afraid of you."

"And you think that's good?"

"I think that's great . . . don't you?"

"No."

"Why not?"

"Because I don't want people to be afraid of me."

"You want them to like you?"

"I want them to leave me alone."

"And don't they? Once they know who you are?"

"No," Clint said. "There's always somebody who thinks they're good with a gun who wants to try me."

"And you kill them!"

"If I can't talk them out of it and it's my only way out, yes."

"I'd kill 'em," Todd said. "If it was me I'd never try to talk them out of it, I'd just kill 'em."

"I want to hear you say that after you've killed your first man."

The waiter came over and took their orders for steak dinners.

"How many men have you killed?" Todd asked.

"I have no idea."

"You don't count?"

"No."

"Come on," Todd said, "don't you notch your gun?"

"That's an awful thing to do to a good gun."

"Are you sure you're the Gunsmith?" Todd asked. "If I hadn't seen you shoot today I'd think you were somebody else."

"I wish I was."

"I don't understand you," Todd said, confused. "Men either fear you or respect you. Ain't that what everybody wants?"

"No!"

"But—"

"Drop it, Todd!" Clint snapped. "It's clear you don't know what you're talking about. You've probably read some dime novels and you think that's the way it's supposed to be in the West. Well, believe me, it's not—but I can see you're not going to believe me, so you're just going to have to find out for yourself."

"And how do I do that?"

"I'm going to take you to Dead Horse Canyon," Clint said, "so you can find out firsthand."

"You know where it is?" Todd demanded. "Why didn't you tell me—"

"I have an idea where it is," Clint said, cutting him off, "but I have some friends who might know exactly where it is. Don't worry, we'll find it."

"And when we do—" Todd said, excited again, but Clint cut him off.

"When we do," Clint said, "I'll let you find out firsthand what it feels like to kill a man. After that maybe I'll listen to your opinions about it."

TEN

They ate their meal in relative silence. Todd's silence was a confused one, Clint's annoyed. He didn't think Todd was a stupid boy. There had to be some way to convince him that killing was not the way to go *without* letting him experience it. He'd been lying when he said he'd take Todd to the canyon and let him kill. He'd just wanted the boy to shut up about it.

And now he had those two idiots Lem and Joe to worry about. All they had to do was go to the hotel and see his name in the register. That was the only confirmation they were going to have as to who he was. If they believed it, they might come after him. If they did, Todd might end up being the one who got hurt.

"Can I get you anything else, sir?" the waiter asked.

"Pie for me," Clint said. "Todd?"

"Me, too."

"Peach?" Clint asked.

"Apple for me," Todd said.

"Coming right up, sir," the waiter said.

They waited for the pie in silence and then Todd said, "My pa's name is Eddie Gilette. I'm Todd Gilette."

"Eddie Gilette," Clint said. "He's been in quite a few

gangs. He's always managed to get out before it was too late."

"He's a survivor," Todd said. "That's what I remember my pa sayin' to me when I was a kid. That's the advice I remember him givin' me. Always be a survivor, Todd. Know when to get out."

"Well," Clint said, "he sure knows how to do that. He's been linked with . . . oh, half a dozen gangs or so. They're all gone, and he's found himself another one."

"He's been ridin' with Trace Atkins for two years," Todd said, "ever since they robbed our town and left me and my ma to take the blame."

"The Atkins gang has pulled some fairly big jobs over that two years, Todd," Clint said. "If they're really hiding out in Dead Horse Canyon they're not going to be easy to get close to."

"I can get in," Todd said.

"How?"

"My pa," he said. "He'll let me in."

"And then how do you get out?"

"I don't care about getting out," Todd said. "I just wanna get in. Once I kill him I don't care what happens."

"Well," Clint said, "maybe you don't, but I sure do. If I'm going to help you I want to be sure I get out alive."

Todd laughed shortly and said, "Why wouldn't you? You're the Gunsmith."

Clint leaned forward and said, "You do know that I can be killed, don't you, Todd?"

"Well, of course."

"I can be shot, just like anybody else."

"No," Todd said, "you'd have to be shot in the back. No one could face you and win."

"Somebody out there can."

"Who?"

"I don't know," Clint said. "I haven't met them, and I

hope I never do, but there's always somebody faster, Todd."

Todd thought about that a moment, and then said, "But just one, right?"

"Well, I don't know . . ."

"If there was more than one," Todd said, "I mean, if you knew there was more than one person who could kill you, wouldn't that scare you?"

"I suppose so."

"Are you ever scared?"

"Sometimes."

Todd's eyes widened.

"Have you ever been scared when facing somebody?"

"All the time."

"But you still do it?"

"You have to do it, Todd," Clint said. "Sometimes you have to do something *because* it scares you."

"Can I tell you something?"

"Sure."

"It scares me, trying to find my father."

"But you're doing it anyway," Clint said. "That's good."

"Do you know what scares me the most about it?"

"What?"

"I'm afraid that when I do see him," Todd said, "I won't be able to kill him. See, I promised my mother, on her grave, that I would kill him for her."

"Todd," Clint said, "do you really think your mother wants you to kill your father for her?"

"Yes."

"What about the guilt you'll carry around after it's done?"

Todd looked confused again.

"Why would I feel guilty about it?"

"Well, because he's your *father*."

"Clint," Todd said, "the only thing I'd feel guilty about is if I can't kill him."

"Todd," Clint said, "you don't expect me to kill him if you can't, do you?"

"No!" Todd said, with conviction. "I don't just want him dead, I want to be the one who kills him. That's important to me. Having you do it wouldn't mean a thing to me, or to my mother."

"I see."

"So you have to promise me you won't kill him."

"Well, all right . . ."

The waiter brought their pie and Todd immediately tucked into his.

"There is something I'll need you to do, though," he said to Clint around a mouthful of pie.

"And what's that?"

Todd swallowed and said, "I'll need you to kill everybody else in the gang."

ELEVEN

"Boy," Clint said, staring across the table, "you have definitely got the wrong idea about me."

Todd stared at Clint and said, "What?"

"The reason I'm going to help you find Dead Horse Canyon," Clint said, "is to keep you alive, and not to kill anyone."

"I told you," Todd said, "I don't care if I come out alive."

"And I told you I do."

"You said you cared that *you* come out alive."

"I care that we both get out alive!"

Todd put his fork down.

"If you're not going to help me kill my pa," Todd said, "what good are you? What are you, afraid? I mean, really afraid?"

"I'm afraid of what killing your own father might do to you," Clint said.

"Why do you even care about me at all?" Todd demanded. "I didn't ask you for your help yesterday and you gave it to me. Now I am asking for your help and you're not going to do it?"

"I'm going to help you, Todd," Clint said, "just not exactly in the way you want me to."

"What are you gonna do, then?"

"I figure we'll find Dead Horse Canyon, and you'll talk to your pa and get some things settled."

"And then what?"

"And then it's up to you from there."

Todd paused, thought it over and said, "I can live with that."

"You can?"

"Yeah."

"Well . . . okay then," Clint said, thinking it was too easy. "We'll leave in the morning, then."

"All right."

"Finish your pie," Clint said. "I'll get you a hotel room for the night, if you like."

"No," Todd said, "the hayloft is good enough. Besides, I have to saddle the horses, remember?"

"Right," Clint said, "I do remember."

"And after we get started," Todd said, "I'll collect wood for the fire, 'cause I can't cook."

"I can," Clint said. "I'm a fair trail cook and I can teach you, if you like."

"Sure," Todd said, "why not? It'll be a way to pass the time until we get to the canyon. About how long do you think that'll take?"

"I'm not sure," Clint said. "You were on the right track by coming to Colorado, but I think it's in the northern part of the state. We'll head up there, find a fairly good size town with a telegraph and make that our base. I can send some telegrams and see what I can dig up."

Todd finished the crumbs of his pie and pushed the dish away.

"What do we do in the meantime?"

"Get some rest," Clint said. "We'll get an early start."

"Could we buy me a handgun?"

"No," Clint said. "I have a couple of extra ones you

can practice on when we camp. If you show any talent with one at all, we can get you one later."

"Okay."

Clint wondered why the boy was being so agreeable. He certainly didn't think he'd changed Todd's mind about killing his father this easily. The boy had to have something up his sleeve.

"Could you teach me something else while we're on the trail?" Todd asked.

"What's that?"

"How to play poker?" Todd asked. "I never learned."

"Sure," Clint said. "I'll see if I can get a couple of decks from the saloon later tonight."

"Great. Thanks. I always wanted to learn."

They left the café and outside Todd said, "I might as well go to the stable and get to know my horse. I'll have to think of a name for him."

"You do that. I'll see you at the livery at first light."

"I'll be ready," Todd said. "Clint . . . thanks for the clothes, the food, the horse . . . everything. I owe you big."

"We'll talk about that when this is all over," Clint said.

"Okay," Todd said. "See you in the morning."

The boy walked off, rifle in hand, and Clint knew that there was still some talking to be done before it was all over.

TWELVE

Clint went to the saloon for a beer and to see if he could get a couple of decks of cards. He walked in, looked around. The place was busy, but Lem and Joe were nowhere in sight. He went to the bar and ordered his beer.

"Maybe you can help me with something else," he said to the bartender when he brought the beer.

"Like what?" the man asked. "You lookin' for company?"

"No," Clint said. "If I was I could take care of that myself."

"Not in this town," the bartender said. "Only good lookin' women in this town are married, or pros."

"Well, that wasn't my question," Clint said. "All I need are a couple of decks of cards."

"Lookin' for a game?"

"I'm leaving town tomorrow," Clint said, "and wanted to take a couple of decks with me."

"I can sell you some new decks, or I can give you some used ones I'd be tossin' out anyway."

"I'll take the used ones."

"Two?"

"That would be plenty."

The bartender reached beneath the bar and came out with two well worn decks of cards that would serve Clint's purpose very nicely.

"There ya go."

"Thanks," Clint said, pocketing them. "I appreciate it."

"You sure about that company?"

"I'm sure."

"Suit yourself."

The bartender walked off and at that moment the fat-bellied sheriff came walking in. He spotted Clint and walked over.

"Still in town?"

"Leaving tomorrow."

"What about the boy?"

"Also leaving tomorrow."

"That's good." The lawman signaled the bartender, who brought over a beer without a word having been spoken.

"When are you leavin'?"

"Early."

"I'd be careful of those two fellas if I was you," the lawman said. "They really didn't seem to like bein' questioned by that kid."

"I know," Clint said. "I had a run-in with them already."

"Oh? I didn't hear no shots."

"I talked them out of any trouble—for now."

"You must talk pretty good."

"When I have to."

The sheriff finished his beer quickly, and looked around the saloon.

"Seems quiet in here," he said. "Got to get on with my rounds. Reckon I won't see you around after tomorrow mornin'."

"I reckon you won't," Clint said, and he didn't think either one of them would be sorry.

"Well, good luck to you," the sheriff said.

Clint nodded and the sheriff left.

"Lard ass," the bartender said, collecting the sheriff's mug. "Comes in here each night, drinks down a beer quick as you please and goes on his way."

"Guess he feels it's part of the job."

"If he does," the bartender said, "it's the only part he does well."

The bartender walked off with the sheriff's empty mug. Clint wondered again—as he often did—why he had dealt himself into a game he hadn't been invited into. It had to have something to do with the way Todd had looked while being pushed across the street by the sheriff. It also had to have something to do with his inability to walk away from someone who obviously needed help, like Todd Gilette.

But would he be able to help him? Certainly not in the way Todd wanted to be helped. It remained to be seen if Clint could accomplish what he was setting out to do— help Todd in a way the boy simply did not want to be helped.

THIRTEEN

"Just because he signed the register 'Clint Adams' don't make him the Gunsmith," Lem said to Joe.

They were sitting in another saloon in town, a smaller one that wasn't so busy—especially since it was near closing time.

"Why else would he sign it that way?"

"Maybe he wants people to think he's the Gunsmith."

"I wouldn't want people thinking I was the Gunsmith," Joe said. "They'd keep tryin' to kill me."

"Okay, so he's the Gunsmith," Lem said. "We should be glad we didn't throw down on him. We'd be dead."

"Yeah," Joe said, "but what if we killed him before he killed us?"

"Did you suddenly become real fast with a gun?"

"Well, no, but there are other ways . . ."

"Like what?"

Joe thought a moment then said, "Well, we could always shoot him in the back. All people would remember is that we killed him."

"Joe, have you ever shot a man in the back?" Lem asked.

"Well, no . . ."

"Neither have I, and I don't intend to start now. Get that idea out of your head right now."

"Okay," Joe said, "so say we just outnumber him."

"We did outnumber him," Lem said, "two to one. It didn't work."

"He had the kid with him, and the kid had a gun," Joe said. "Besides, what if we outnumber him more than two to one?"

"Like how many?"

"Four, maybe five to one?"

"And we kill him head on?"

"Right?"

"Where do we get the help?"

"We both know people."

"What if he manages to kill one of us?"

"We both know people we don't like that much."

"But what if it's you or me he kills?" Lem asked.

Joe frowned.

"Clearly, we have to think this over more carefully," Lem said.

"Okay, so—"

"What do you say," Lem asked, "that we just forget about him?"

"Did you forget that he's looking for Dead Horse Canyon?" Joe asked.

"Lots of people have been looking for Dead Horse Canyon for years, Joe," Lem said. "They haven't found it."

"We have friends in Dead Horse Canyon," Joe said. "We have a responsibility to protect them."

"But not to get killed doing it."

Joe hesitated a moment, then said, "You got a point there."

They both fell silent for a few moments, and then Lem said, "Okay, so we give it some more thought."

FOURTEEN

There were three houses in Dead Horse Canyon. One was used as a bunkhouse. Another was used by whoever the leader of the gang was at the time. These days it was Trace Atkins. The third house was used by the leader's second in command, and a few other left- and right-hand men.

Eddie Gilette came out of the third house and looked up at the sky. He looked at the canyon walls, couldn't see the men who were on watch, but knew they were there. No one could get in or out of the canyon without being seen.

He smelled coffee and bacon. Somebody had started breakfast, so he wasn't the first one up.

He looked over at Trace Atkins's house. He knew that Trace was in there with Belinda. There were three women in the canyon, all there for the pleasure of the men. There was no place for the women to live, so at night each woman went to bed with a man. Usually, it was a different man each night, because the women were there for everyone. Nobody was supposed to be forming any relationships. Lately, however, Belinda had been going to bed with Trace more than anyone else—and who was going to say anything? Trace was the leader.

Gilette followed his nose to the breakfast. A man named Starling was standing over the fire. There was a huge pot of coffee going and more than one frying pan with bacon in it.

"Mornin'," Starling said. "Coffee?"

"Yup."

Gilette held the tin cup while Starling used two hands to pour it full.

"Breakfast'll be ready in a few minutes."

"Fine."

Gilette drank his coffee hot, without making any attempt to cool it off. He liked it that way, so hot it peeled the skin off the palate of most men—but not him.

He walked over to where the horses were, saw that they were all secure. He looked over at Atkins's house again. Trace was usually the first or second one up. Today he would do no better than third, unless Belinda kept him in bed longer than that.

Gilette was starting to worry about Atkins. Trace had been leader of the gang for three years now. That was a long time. Gilette had been part of this gang for longer than that. He was second in command when it was the Decatur gang, when it was the Foster gang, and even when it was the Starling gang. That's right, at one time Starling was the leader, but Atkins had taken the gang away from him, and kept him around to make breakfast and run errands. It was a smart thing to do, keep the old leader around and make him do menial tasks while the rest of the gang watched. Atkins was a smart man, but lately he wasn't making such smart decisions, and Gilette was worried.

The thing that worried Gilette was the same thing that always worried him when it looked like a leader was losing his ability to lead—who would be next? Gilette never wanted to be the leader, but he had always managed to find someone he could talk into it, someone who had some leadership ability and just needed some guidance.

At the moment, though, there was no one in Dead Horse Canyon who could fill that bill.

It was beginning to look like, once and for all, Eddie Gilette might have to step forward.

Trace Atkins turned Belinda over in bed and admired the twin cheeks of her ass. The pale orbs were just this side of being too big, but as long as they stayed on "this" side she had a perfect butt.

He ran his erect penis along the cleft between them and she moaned as she felt his hot column of flesh gliding over her. She spread her legs then, as wide as she could. He slid his cock down until it was poking up between her legs. He didn't slide into her ass, but into her hot, wet pussy. He loved the way it felt to be inside a woman from this angle, and Belinda was one woman who liked it this way as much as he did. Most of the other women he'd been with—and certainly the others in Dead Horse Canyon—had no imagination. They just liked to lie on their back and spread their legs. Not Belinda. Once Atkins was inside her she started rocking back and forth, sliding him in and out of her, wetting him thoroughly, moaning and crying out. He gripped her hips and pulled her to him so he could drive into her harder and harder. He felt her hand slide between her legs and touch both of them there, making her catch her breath, and then he knew she was squeezing her own breasts and nipples with one hand while supporting her weight with the other. He slid out of her then and turned her over so he could see her breasts. They were large and pale, with big brown nipples. He slid up so he could put his penis between them. She squeezed them together so he could fuck them, and every time his dick came near her mouth she stuck her tongue out to take a swipe at him.

"Come on, Trace baby," she said, "come on, give it to me . . ."

She liked being with Trace Atkins because he didn't just dump her on her back and take her. When it came to sex they had the same ideas, and she felt she had finally found a man she wanted to be with forever—if she could just get him to leave this gang behind him.

He began to move faster and faster between her tits and when he was ready to explode he moved up and slid himself between her sweet lips. She sucked him, then, and when he exploded she kept sucking and sucking, hoping that she was actually sucking him away from this life he was leading.

"Come on, Trace," she said, just a few moments later, watching him get dressed, "the time is now."

"I can't Belinda," Atkins said. "The men still need me."

"They don't need you," she said. "Let them be on their own for a change. I need you, Trace, and you need me."

He looked at her, lying on her back, still naked and wet from him, and said, "Yeah, I do, Belinda."

"So you'll do it?" she asked. "You'll leave here with me?"

She saw it in his eyes, he was this close to saying yes, and then he said, "I've got to go. I'll see you later."

He went out the door without giving her the answer she wanted, but she wasn't disappointed. She almost had him, that time.

Almost.

FIFTEEN

Trace Atkins found Eddie Gilette hunched by the fire, eating breakfast. He looked around, didn't see anyone else up besides Gilette and Starling. As he approached the fire Starling handed him a cup of coffee. Atkins thought he had the former gang leader trained well. He hunched down next to Gilette, waiting for Starling to hand him a plate for breakfast.

"Mornin', Eddie."

"Trace."

Starling handed Atkins his breakfast and the man started eating, setting his coffee down on the ground between his feet.

"Belinda last night?" Gilette asked.

"Yeah. So?"

"Nothin'."

"You got a problem with Belinda?"

"No."

"With me and Belinda?"

Gilette looked at Atkins, then looked away.

"You know the rules, Trace."

"I can break the rules, Eddie," Atkins said. "I'm the ramrod of this outfit, remember?"

Gilette just nodded his head. Atkins had conveniently forgotten who *made* him the ramrod of the outfit.

"There's other women here, you know," Atkins said.

"It's not about women, Eddie," Gilette said. "I've had plenty of women."

"That's right," Atkins said. "You had a wife, didn't you? And a kid. A son. Whatever happened to him?"

"I don't know."

"Don't you ever wonder?"

Gilette looked at Trace Atkins.

"You thinkin' about havin' kids, Trace?" he asked. "Maybe with Belinda?"

"What if I was?"

"Not a good idea," Gilette said. "Not for men in our business. I found out about that firsthand."

"What would you tell your kid, if you saw him now?" Atkins asked. "If he rode in here right now, what would you tell him?"

"I'd tell him that I'm not apologizin' for anything," Gilette said. "I lived my life the way I saw fit. A man shouldn't have to apologize for that."

"Oh, I agree, Eddie," Trace Atkins said. "I truly agree."

Gilette realized then that he had painted himself into a corner. He couldn't criticize the younger man for his decisions without making himself sound like a hypocrite.

"The men are getting restless," he said, changing the subject. "They're wonderin' when we're gonna go out and pull the next job."

"I'm workin' on it, Eddie," Atkins said. "I'm workin' on it. If any of them have any complaints, tell 'em to come to me with them."

"I'll do that, Trace," Gilette said.

Atkins was a big man, good with a gun, still young— in his mid-thirties. He could head up this gang for a long time, make a real name for himself. All he had to do was not get hooked up to a woman—to the wrong woman.

Gilette was in his early forties. He'd been the back-bone of half a dozen gangs, served under that many leaders, and he thought Atkins could be the best of them. He looked across the fire at Starling, who was concentrating on his cooking. Starling had been a decent leader, but he'd been too old to start with, and when Atkins had come along he couldn't fight him. Now in his fifties Starling's life was over, except for making coffee and bacon, and dinner later in the day, usually beans or a stew.

Gilette wondered what he'd be doing in ten years, when he was Starling's age. Would he still be number two in some gang? Was it, in fact, time for him to start thinking about actually being number one? If he wanted to—or had to—could he take this gang away from Trace Atkins?

He'd been telling Atkins the truth when he said he'd tell his boy that he didn't apologize for anything. He'd lived his life just the way he'd always wanted to, and he would go on doing just that.

The door to the first house opened, the biggest one, which was used as a bunkhouse. Several men came staggering out, hawking and spitting and coughing, clearing their lungs for the new day. They came over to the fire, greeted both Atkins and Gilette and demanded their breakfast from Starling.

The time for talking had passed. It was time to do some thinking.

Belinda Carter looked out the window and saw Atkins and Eddie Gilette talking by the fire. There had been a time when she thought Gilette was her way out of Dead Horse Canyon. She still thought he was the strongest and smartest man in the gang, but it was Trace Atkins she'd be able to sway, not Gilette. Atkins was younger, and had not been riding with gangs for as long as Gilette had. Also, Gilette had a wife somewhere, and maybe even a kid. She'd slept with Gilette, and she knew he'd been with a lot of women before. It was in the way he made love. The others just took their own pleasures and went to sleep. Gilette was different, he knew how to treat a woman when he wanted to—but again, it was Trace she would be able to control through sex, not Eddie Gilette.

She often wondered why Eddie Gilette didn't just take over the gang, be the boss for a change. Maybe he'd do just that once she took Trace away from here. She only needed a few more nights to work on him—maybe even one more night—and she was sure she could convince him to leave. The only trouble she might have would come from Gilette. Atkins was the boss, but he listened to Gilette, respected him.

She'd know real soon, though—real soon.

SIXTEEN

Clint and Todd Gilette rode out of Broken Branch that morning. The boy had both his horse and Clint's saddled and ready to go when Clint arrived at the livery.

"I know how to saddle a horse," Todd said when Clint started checking his saddle.

"Only a fool doesn't double-check everything, Todd," Clint said. "Remember that."

"Okay."

They mounted up and rode out of town, heading north.

"Tell me again how you decided to look in Colorado for Dead Horse Canyon, Todd," Clint said.

"It was something my mother said," Todd replied. "That's all. It took me a long time to get here. I had to keep stopping along the way to take odd jobs to make money. It's taken me just as long to get this far in Colorado."

"Well," Clint said, "things'll go a little faster from now on, now that you've got a sponsor."

"A what?"

Clint smiled and said, "Somebody to pay the bills."

"Oh, yeah."

• • •

They stopped to camp just before dark that evening and Clint decided to see how well Todd would listen and do his chores. He told the boy to collect the wood for the fire, and then to see to the horses.

"I said I'd do the wood," Todd reminded him.

"You'll have to do whatever I say, Todd," Clint said. "Only one person can be in charge."

"And it'll be you because you're older?" Todd demanded.

"Older's got nothing to do with it," Clint said. "I'm more experienced than you are."

Todd couldn't argue with that, but that didn't mean that he went about his chores without grumbling. In that respect he was apparently just like every other teenage boy Clint had ever met.

Once Todd had collected the wood Clint started the fire and began preparing dinner. By the time Todd had seen to the horses, it was time to eat. When he came to the fire Clint handed him a plate of bacon and beans.

"These beans are good," Todd said, around a mouthful.

"It's the bacon," Clint said.

"Can I have some coffee?" Todd asked.

"Do you usually drink coffee?"

"What else is there to drink?"

"Water."

Todd made a face.

"I'd rather have coffee."

"Suit yourself."

Clint poured him a cup and handed it to him. The boy drank it as if it was water. Clint was surprised it didn't burn his mouth.

After dinner Todd surprised Clint by asking, "What do you want me to do now, Clint?"

"Just relax," Clint said, deciding to give the boy a break. "I'll clean up here and then we can turn in."

"So early?"

"Got to get an early start on the day when you're on the trail, Todd," Clint said. "What's the point of staying up late, anyway? There's nothing to do but look up at the sky."

"I like looking at the sky."

"You can do that from your bedroll."

"How about setting a watch?" Todd asked. "I can take a turn, you know."

"What are we watching for?" Clint asked. "We're looking for somebody, somebody's not looking for us."

"I just thought you'd always be careful."

"You're right," Clint said. "I am. I usually sleep pretty light when I'm traveling alone."

"See? If I stood watch you could sleep more soundly, then you could relieve me and I could do the same."

"All right, Todd," Clint said. "If that's what you want to do. We could both use a few hours of deep sleep rather than twice as many hours of light sleep. Do you want the first watch, or the second?"

"I'll take the first," Todd said. "I'm not sleepy."

"All right," Clint said. After all, the boy was younger and probably didn't feel as tired as Clint did.

Clint cleaned the plates and put on a fresh pot of coffee. He and Todd had another cup each before Clint rolled himself up in his blanket to go to sleep.

"Make sure you don't look directly into the fire," Clint said. "It'll ruin your night vision."

"Okay," Todd said. He reached for his rifle and set it across his knees.

"If you hear anything don't hesitate. Wake me up right away."

"I will," Todd said. "Don't worry. Thanks for trusting me."

"We're out here together, Todd," Clint said. "We've got to watch each other's backs."

"Yessir," Todd said, "we sure do. G'night."

"Night, Todd," Clint said. "Don't forget to wake me in four hours."

"I won't forget."

Clint slept lightly for about an hour before letting himself drift off into a deeper sleep.

SEVENTEEN

When Todd gently prodded Clint awake—almost as if he was afraid he *would* wake him—they exchanged places with only a few words.

"Anything?" Clint asked.

"No, nothing," Todd said. "I didn't see or hear nothing."

"Go to sleep," Clint said, and poured himself a cup of coffee.

As he had told Todd there was little to do beyond staring at the sky, so he drank his coffee and looked at the stars. It was very quiet out. The horses were not even making a sound, which was good. If there was any sort of four-legged critter out there the horses would let them know. For the two-legged kind they would just have to be on the alert.

In truth, Clint had intended to stand watch for part of the night, but he hadn't intended to make Todd do the same. He was glad the boy had come up with the idea all by himself. He still, however, thought that Todd was just stringing him along when it came to certain things. He was sure the boy was smart enough to tell him what he thought he wanted to hear so he wouldn't keep lecturing him about killing his own father. Clint knew that when they did find Dead Horse Canyon he'd have a fight on his hands to keep the boy from fulfilling his promise to his mother. Todd wasn't thinking about the rest of his life, so how could he be expected to believe that such an act would ruin it?

Clint poured the remnants of his coffee from his cup into the fire and reached for the pot. He was surprised to find it almost empty. Todd must have drank a lot of coffee while on watch. Clint made a fresh pot, and sat back with a full cup to contemplate the stars, and the future of a boy who didn't want one.

At one point during the night Clint heard Todd stirring, and then the boy stared to whimper in his sleep, sounding very much like a small boy having a nightmare. There was nothing Clint could do, though. To wake the boy and assure him that everything was all right would have embarrassed him. He had to leave him alone and let him work things out for himself in his dreams. After a while the whimpering stopped and Todd settled back into a deep sleep.

When first light began to touch the sky Clint put some bacon into a frying pan and made still another fresh pot of coffee. The combination of smells served to wake Todd up and he got to his feet much easier than Clint had when he'd awakened. Clint envied his young bones and legs.

"Boy, I'm hungry," Todd said.

"Breakfast is just about ready," Clint said. "It's a light one, just some bacon and coffee. I think we might come to a town today. We can stop for a better meal."

"We don't have to stop on my account," Todd said. "I can eat trail food as long as you can."

"Then we'll stop for me," Clint said, "because I'm starting to get a craving for a piece of pie—which we can't get here on the trail."

Todd saddled the horses while Clint doused the fire and broke camp. They mounted up and started riding north once again.

Later that afternoon Clint reined his horse in and turned in his saddle to look behind them.

"What's wrong?" Todd asked.

"Nothing," Clint said. "Just a feeling."

"We're being followed?"

"Maybe."

"By who?"

"I don't know."

"Those two from Broken Branch?"

Clint looked at Todd.

"Maybe, but I wouldn't think they'd come after us," Clint said. "Not just the two of them, anyway. Todd, just how upset did they get when you started asking questions about Dead Horse Canyon?"

"Real upset," Todd said. "I had the feeling they knew where it was, and knew who was there. I still think they did."

"Well, if that's the case," Clint said, "you'd think they'd try to get there ahead of us to warn their friends we were coming, rather than trail along behind us."

"Maybe it ain't them," Todd said. "Maybe it's somebody else."

"Could be anybody," Clint said, "for any reason." He turned in his saddle to face forward. "Or maybe it's no one."

"If you say there's somebody," Todd said, "I believe you. Didn't you tell me a man pays attention to his instincts?"

"Ah," Clint said, "you listen to me when I tell you something, huh?"

"Sometimes," Todd said, with a shrug.

"Well," Clint said, "I guess that's better than nothing. Let's get moving. I still want a piece of pie."

They'd seen a sign about an hour before for a town called Blissful. Clint was curious to see if the place would live up to its name.

EIGHTEEN

Blissful appeared to be small and quiet as they rode into town. They had no intention of staying any longer than it took to have a meal and a piece of pie. Their supplies were fine, so they didn't need to stock up on anything. They were carrying all they needed in two canvas sacks, tied one each to their saddlehorns. This was a practice Clint used in order to avoid the extra burden of a pack-horse.

They found a likely looking café right on the main street and tied their horses off in front. This was something Clint had never had to do with Duke, as the big black gelding would never have walked off. His new horse, Eclipse, was not quite that reliable yet, although the Darley Arabian had done everything else that had been asked of him.

They went inside and were seated immediately, as it was a time that was between meals in Blissful. They both settled on beef stew and coffee.

"He drinks coffee?" the waitress asked, indicating Todd.

"What about it?" Todd asked, bristling.

"No offense, son," the middle-aged woman said, "but you look a little young for coffee."

"Okay, then," Todd said, "bring me some whiskey."

She made a face and said, "Two beef stews and coffees coming up."

"Don't worry about it," Clint said. "You got plenty of time to get older. As soon as you start to shave that'll stop."

Todd didn't comment, but it was clear what he was thinking. He didn't expect to get old enough to shave. Clint wondered why this journey of his had to be so suicidal? Why couldn't he think of accomplishing what he wanted to accomplish and getting out alive?

The stew came and was good. From where Clint sat he could see out the window and the door. He was wondering if whoever was following them would actually follow them into town. From his vantage point he'd be able to see if anyone rode into town after them.

"You still think we're being followed?" Todd asked, noticing that Clint's attention was on the street.

"Just a feeling," Clint said. "I still haven't seen anything."

"Think those two would be good enough to trail us without being seen?" the boy asked.

"I don't know what those two would be good at," Clint said.

"Well, they weren't so good at facing you."

"Maybe gunplay just isn't what they're good at," Clint said. "Maybe their talents lie on the trail."

"So what do we do now?"

"Eat," Clint said, "just eat."

After the stew, which was pretty good, they had their pie: peach for Clint, apple for Todd.

"Why do you like apple pie so much?" Clint asked.

"My mom used to make apple pies all the time."

"Oh."

"Why do you like peach so much?" Todd asked. "Did your mom make it for you?"

"No," Clint said, "I discovered it a few years ago and just really liked it."

"Do you have any family?"

"Nope."

"No wife or kid?"

"Uh uh," Clint said. "No."

"How come?"

"I travel much too much to get married," Clint said. "It wouldn't be fair to a wife or a child."

Todd sulked for a moment. Clint knew he was thinking he wished his own father had thought that way.

"Are we getting right back on the trail?" the boy asked, after a moment.

"Unless there's something you need, yeah," Clint said.

"No," Todd said, "nothing. What about those telegrams you said you were going to send?"

"That won't be for a while," Clint said. "Besides, this town doesn't have a telegraph wire."

Todd picked up his rifle while Clint paid the bill and they walked outside together. No one had ridden past the café since they went inside, but that didn't mean that no one had come into town at all. Clint looked both ways, then checked windows and rooftops.

"Are we going?" Todd asked.

"We're going," Clint said. "Mount up."

Clint watched Todd mount up then swung into the saddle himself. He wondered if his feelings of being followed, or watched, were just figments of his imagination, or if his instincts were once again warning him.

He rode a little behind Todd so he could watch the boy's back, but his own back itched because no one was watching it. He didn't know if the two men—Lem and Joe was all he knew them by—were backshooters or not.

His initial impression of them had been that they were talkers, not doers, but he really hadn't seen enough of them to know for sure.

They rode out of Blissful, still with no idea if the town lived up to its name or not. It wasn't something that he would be coming back to find out. He decided that this would be their last stop in a town unless they were desperate for supplies. He certainly didn't need the extra tension of a possible ambush from an alley or a rooftop. There was enough to deal with on the trail.

NINETEEN

Lem and Joe kept well behind Clint and Todd, not so much following them as tracking them.

"If they're going to Dead Horse Canyon," Joe asked, "why don't we just get there ahead of them?"

"What if they don't find it?" Lem asked.

"Then there's no harm done."

"No," Lem said, "we've decided to kill the Gunsmith, right?"

"Right."

"And before we left Broken Branch we sent telegrams out for help, right?" Lem asked.

"Right."

"So we just have to track them until that help finds us."

"How they gonna do that?"

"I figure if Adams is actually on the right track," Lem said, "he and the kid are gonna have to come to Dortville. We can all meet up there."

"Dortville ain't much of a town," Joe said.

"It's the closest one to the canyon," Lem said. "If they get there, then they can almost stumble into the canyon. That's where we'll take 'em."

The first night Lem and Joe camped miles away from Clint and the boy.

"I can smell their bacon," Lem complained, while they munched on beef jerky.

"We ain't makin' any smells of our own," Lem said. "Not while we're trailin' them."

"And coffee," Joe muttered. "I can smell coffee."

"Eat your jerky," Lem said, "and shut up."

When Clint and Todd rode into Blissful, Lem and Joe stayed outside of town.

"I gotta have somethin' decent to eat, Lem," Joe said.

"We'll wait for them to leave town, then we'll go in and eat," Lem said. "They won't get too far ahead of us that way."

"They'll never lose you, Lem," Joe said. "Not the way you can track."

"You ain't got to butter me up, Joe," Lem said. "I already said we'll stop and eat in Blissful."

"Wasn't butterin' ya up," Joe muttered. "You are a good tracker."

"Okay," Lem said, "I'm sorry. Thanks for the compliment."

"Yer welcome."

"Now shut up!"

TWENTY

"Smell that?" Clint asked.

Todd lifted his head and sniffed the air.

"What?"

"A camp."

"How can you tell?"

"Just put your head up and breathe, don't sniff," Clint said. "Let it come to you."

Todd did as he was told and in minutes he smelled it.

"Is that bacon?"

"And coffee."

They'd been on the trail three days now and, according to Clint, would soon be in a town called Dirtville. Its actual name, for some unknown reason was Dortville, but everyone called it Dirtville. That was where he intended to hole up for a while and send out some telegrams.

At the moment, though, they were only about a half hour from camping themselves when Clint smelled the other camp.

"Could it be them?" Todd asked. "Whoever's following us?"

"No," Clint said, "the wind's not at our backs. The smell is coming from ahead of us."

"So what do we do?"

"Let's keep going," Clint said, "and see what we can find."

Todd took his rifle from his scabbard and settled it across his thighs.

"That's not a bad idea, Todd," Clint said, "but don't be too quick to bring it to bear. Take your cues from me, got it?"

"Yes, sir."

"Don't ever fire unless I do."

"Okay."

They rode for a few minutes and then Todd asked, "What if I see somebody about to shoot you in the back?"

"Well," Clint said, "in that case, use your own judgment."

As they got closer to the camp the smells became stronger. Soon, they could even hear sounds. Voices, horses and even . . .

"Are those pots rattling?" Todd asked.

"Sounds like it."

"More than one person, then?"

"Yes."

"What do we do when we find them?"

"Let's just wait and see."

Clint halted their progress and told Todd to dismount.

"Wait here."

"I want to come."

"Can you walk without making a sound?"

Todd hesitated.

"Wait here."

Clint handed Todd the reins of his horse and started forward on foot. He could make out the voices now as those of a man and a woman. Occasionally they got louder, as if they were arguing. Then, finally, he saw them, camped in a clearing just a little ways ahead of him. He stopped to watch and listen.

There were two of them, a man and a woman, both young, maybe in their twenties. They weren't arguing so much as the woman was lighting into the man. She was pretty, with a good shape beneath a cheap dress and long blonde hair. The man was tall and thin, still had some filling out to do. He was bent over the fire while the woman was complaining to him.

". . . don't know why you insisted on dragging me out here," she was saying. "This is Godforsaken country, for sure. You said we were going to get a house near a decent town—"

"We are—"

"That's what you call this?" she demanded, cutting him off. "You know, mother warned me . . ."

Clint moved away then, not wanting to hear anymore. When he got back to Todd the boy was waiting anxiously.

"Well, who is it?"

"Just a young couple camped ahead," Clint said. "They have a wagon full of goods, maybe even furniture. Sounds like they just got married and are looking for a place to live."

"So what do we do?" Todd asked. "Go around them?"

"I'd do that if we weren't running low on coffee and food," Clint said. "I can't resist the smell of that coffee. Let's ride into their camp and see if they'll offer us anything."

"Okay," Todd said. "Maybe they have something else to eat other than beans, too."

"Maybe," Clint said, accepting back Eclipse's reins. "Let's mount up and find out."

Clint had another reason for wanting to bust in on the

young couple. He had been able to see the young man's face while the woman was berating him. He believed that by interrupting them they might even be saving the woman's life, because that young fella looked just about ready to kill his new bride.

TWENTY-ONE

"Hello the camp!" Clint called.

He had no idea how this young couple would react to visitors. He didn't know if the man was an experienced traveler. It seemed obvious the woman was not. He didn't want to scare them into doing anything foolish.

"Who's there?" the man's voice called out.

"Just a traveler who smelled your coffee," Clint said. "We're out and could use some."

He heard the woman's voice say, ". . . don't . . ." shrilly, but didn't catch the rest.

"Come ahead," the man called. "We have it aplenty."

Clint and Todd rode their horses to the edge of the camp and then dismounted. The appearance of a man and a boy seemed to put the man at ease, but the woman was standing behind him and scowling at them.

"A lady as pretty as you are, ma'am, shouldn't frown like that," Clint said.

"My wife is wary of strangers," the man said.

"Then she's a smart woman," Clint said. "Pretty and smart. You're a lucky man, sir."

"Come on into camp, mister," the young man said. "My name's Judd Butler, this here's my misses, Annabelle."

Clint and Todd walked closer. Todd was staring at Annabelle Butler, his throat dry. He'd never seen anyone so pretty before.

"My name's Clint Adams," Clint said, "and this is Todd Gilette."

"Is he your son?' Annabelle asked.

"No, ma'am," Clint said. "He's a fine boy, but we're just traveling together."

Clint wasn't sure yet how much he wanted to tell the Butlers.

"Clint's helpin' me find my father," Todd said.

Clint waited for Todd to add, ". . . and then I'm gonna kill him," but thankfully he did not.

"Well, you're welcome to share our fire, our food, and our camp, if you've a mind to," Judd said.

"That's very kind of you, Mr. Butler."

"Just Judd," Butler said. "Annabelle, we got guests for supper."

"A-all right," she said, contritely. It was hard to believe looking at her that just a little while ago she'd been berating him mercilessly.

"Todd," Clint said, "why don't you take our horses and tie them off over there by Mr.—by Judd's team?"

"Okay."

Clint looked at Judd and said, "Let's get better acquainted before you invite us to stay, Judd. Just makes good sense."

"Yes, sir," Judd said, "it does."

Judd poured Clint a cup of coffee and handed it to him. Annabelle went over to their wagon to get something out of the back. Todd was over by the horses, tying them off.

"I know who you are, Mr. Adams," Judd said.

"You do?"

"Yes, sir."

"Does that mean you want me to leave?"

"No, sir. I'm just . . . sayin'.."

Clint looked across the fire at Judd. He couldn't have been more than seven or eight years older than Todd.

"Can I ask you a question, Judd?"

"Sure."

"Why would a young man like you choose to get married?"

Judd looked around and then said, "Can I tell you the truth?"

Clint didn't know what he'd done in such a short time to deserve the truth, but he said, "Sure."

"I sorta been wonderin' that myself lately. I mean, I love Annabelle. She's beautiful, you can see that."

"Yes, I can."

"She's just . . ."

"Mean?"

Judd looked surprised, then said, "Well . . . yeah, sometimes. Why is that?"

"I don't know, Judd," Clint said. "I've never been married, myself, and don't suppose I ever will be. I don't spend that much time with women to be able to figure them out . . . if you know what I mean."

"I believe I do, sir," Judd said, "but I just can't be that kind of man . . . no offense meant."

"None taken."

At that point both Annabelle and Todd returned to the fire.

"We'll need some more water, Judd, so I can make more stew than I intended," she said.

"Todd can go with you," Clint said, "or go get it for you."

"Yes, ma'am," Todd said, eagerly. "Uh, whichever you prefer."

"All right, Todd," Annabelle said. "Come with me and I'll show you where the waterhole is."

"Yes, ma'am."

"You see?" Judd said, as Todd and Annabelle walked away.

"See what, son?"

"Todd's what? Sixteen. Seventeen?"

"Sixteen."

"And he's already in love with Annabelle," Judd said. "I reckon that's why I married her."

"Because you love her?"

"Yes, sir."

Clint sipped his coffee and said, "I guess that's a damn good reason, Judd."

"Yes, sir," Judd said, "it is."

TWENTY-TWO

Annabelle's stew turned out to be better than anything Clint had had in a while, and better than anything Todd had ever had.

"Ma'am," Todd said, "that was better than anything my ma ever made."

"Why, Todd, how sweet," Annabelle said. "Thank you."

Todd and Annabelle had returned from fetching the water laughing and apparently very comfortable with each other. She seemed very little like the shrew Clint had first thought her, and now he was wondering if he had judged her too harshly, too quickly.

"More coffee, anyone?" she asked.

"Please," Clint said, extending his cup.

"Judd?" she asked.

"Yes, thank you."

"And Todd?"

"Thanks, ma'am." Todd especially liked Annabelle because she didn't treat him like a child. It was causing him to get ideas that might later get him into trouble.

"I have to go to the waterhole to properly wash these things," Annabelle said to Todd. "Would you help me?

It's pretty dark out there now, and I don't want to fall in."

"Sure."

Todd quickly got to his feet and wiped his hands on his thighs, then followed Annabelle out of camp.

"It's getting worse," Judd said, scowling.

"What is?"

"Todd. He's really smitten with her."

"He's just a kid, Judd. Don't worry."

"Annabelle's, she's . . . kinda funny, sometimes."

"How do you mean?"

"She likes to . . . play."

"You mean, she might deliberately lead Todd on?"

"Maybe."

"Well," Clint said, "Todd and I will be leaving in the morning. I don't think you have to worry about anything."

"Where are you headed, Mr. Adams?"

"North," Clint said. "Eventually a town called Dortville."

"I've heard of that," Judd said. "Don't they call it Dirtville?"

"Some people do. Where are you headed?"

"We left Denver to find a place to live," Judd said. "I don't know how far we're gonna go."

"I see. Well, I'm sure you'll find something."

Judd looked off in the direction Annabelle and Todd had taken, then looked back at Clint.

At the waterhole Annabelle had a plan. She wanted to make Judd jealous, but she also thought Todd was kind of cute, and she was sure he was a virgin. While they were cleaning the utensils in the waterhole she made a point of brushing up against him with her hips and breasts. Todd thought he was going to explode, being that close to her, touching her, smelling her . . .

"Ooh," Annabelle said, and made like she was going to fall into the waterhole. Todd grabbed her around the waist and pulled her back. She immediately grabbed his hands so he couldn't take them away, and she pressed her warm body back against him. She could feel his erection through his trousers and was surprised to find him so . . . developed. He seemed to be even bigger than Judd.

"Thank you, Todd," she said, rubbing her hands over his arms, "I almost fell in. I could have caught my death of cold."

"That's okay."

He tried to take his arms away but she held them tight. His nose was buried in her fragrant hair. She was pressing her firm, round little buttocks right into his swollen crotch.

"I . . . we better get back . . ."

"I like your arms around me," she said. "They're strong."

"Well—"

"Don't you like me?"

"Well, yes, ma'am. I like you fine."

"Just fine?"

"I like you a lot, ma'am."

"Annabelle," she said. "Just call be Annabelle."

"Annabelle."

She turned her head so she could look at him. Her mouth was so close to his. She moistened it with her tongue. She had the most beautiful eyes and skin he had ever seen, and even the smell of her breath was sweet.

"Todd?"

"Y-yes?"

"Would you like to kiss me?"

"Um, yes, ma'am, but . . ."

"But what?"

"You're married."

"Judd won't know," she whispered, her mouth almost on his. "It'll just be a kiss. No harm."

"Ma'am—"

"How old are you, Todd?"

"Sixteen," he said. "Almost seventeen."

"I'm twenty-three. Do you think that's very old?"

"N-no, not at all."

"Have you ever kissed a girl?"

"No, ma'am."

"You have a very nice mouth," she said. "I bet lots of girls would like to kiss you." And then she did something that shocked him. She stuck her tongue out and licked his mouth. He thought he'd die right there.

"Annabelle—" he said, and then she kissed him. Her mouth on his was the sweetest thing he'd ever tasted, and then her tongue was in his mouth and he wasn't sure what to do, so he just put his in hers.

"Oh, Todd," she said, pulling her mouth away, "you have too kissed a girl before."

"No, I haven't," he said, "honest. You're my first, Annabelle."

"Then you just simply are the best kisser I ever—" She stopped and removed his arms from her waist. "I think we better go back to camp before I do something I'm sorry for."

"Annabelle—"

"No," she said, "I can't trust myself, Todd. I—I can't."

And she hurried back to camp. Todd was afraid to move, afraid that he'd mess his pants the way he had once or twice in his bed, after certain kinds of dreams. He waited a few moments, and then ran after her, not wanting her to stumble back to camp in the dark alone.

Todd Gilette was hopelessly in love with a young woman who was just playing with him.

TWENTY-THREE

Judd pulled Annabelle aside after she returned from the waterhole with Todd.

"You're playin' games with that boy," he said.

"Harmless game," she said. "What's the big deal?"

"The big deal is that's Clint Adams he's ridin' with," Judd said. "The Gunsmith. Do you understand?"

"How do you know—"

"I know," Judd said. "They're gonna stay with us tonight and then be on their way. For once in your life have some control."

"If you could satisfy me," she said, "I would."

"Annabelle, so help me God—"

"What?" she asked. "What will you do? Kill me?"

Judd glared at her, then turned and walked away from her. Someday maybe that's just what he would do, kill her.

But not today.

Clint took Todd aside and said, "Be careful of the woman."

"She's wonderful."

Too late, Clint thought. The kid already had stars in his eyes and a bulge in his pants.

"Todd, she's married."

"We didn't do nothin'," Todd said, looking guilty.

"Look," Clint said, "we're leaving tomorrow. Just stay away from her tonight. Don't look for trouble."

"Clint . . . I think she likes me," Todd said. "I don't think she's happy with her husband."

"Todd," Clint said, "you're sixteen years old."

"Almost seventeen."

"She's just playing games."

"She ain't like that," Todd said, angrily. "Why don't you like her?"

"Son," Clint said, "you're losing sight of why you're out here."

"Ain't you the one who told me I shouldn't kill my own father?" Todd demanded.

"Yes, but—"

"What would you rather I do," Todd asked. "Go away with Annabelle or kill my old man?"

"Todd," Clint said, "I think there's more chance of the second happening than the first."

"You don't think a woman could love me?" Todd asked.

"Not this woman, Todd, no," Clint said. "There are plenty of other girls out there who are your age, unmarried—"

"They're not Annabelle."

Clint felt like he was banging his head against a stone wall.

"Look, Todd," he said, trying again, "her husband knows that she likes to play games. He warned me."

"And you believe him? She ain't happy with him," Todd said. "Why would he tell you something good about her?"

"Look, Todd— Oh, forget it. Get some sleep. In the

morning if you want to give up on Dead Horse Canyon, you just let me know."

Todd glared at Clint, then turned and went to get his bedroll. Instead of putting it down by the fire he stalked off into the shadows with it.

Clint laid his bedroll by the fire and poured himself some coffee. He'd made a mistake bringing Todd into this camp. This young couple was not at all what they seemed to be when he first saw them. Something was going on, and he didn't want to stick around to find out what it was. In the morning they'd get up early and get away from here.

If he could get Todd to leave a woman like Annabelle.

"We sleep in the wagon," Judd had told Clint before turning in. "We'll see you in the morning."

Clint was lying on his side, awake, when he saw Annabelle step down from the wagon. She looked around, then hurried off into the shadows. Clint got up and walked to the wagon. From inside he could hear the even breathing of a man in a deep sleep. Annabelle had waited for her husband to fall asleep, and now she was off looking for trouble.

Clint went into the shadows where she had gone.

Annabelle, when away from the camp, circled around to where she knew Todd was lying.

"Todd," she said, in a loud whisper.

Todd, who was already awake, sat up and said, "Annabelle."

She came and knelt in front of him.

"I couldn't stay away," she told him. "Not after that kiss."

She put her hand on his crotch, leaned forward and kissed him again. While kissing him she undid his pants and drew him out, fully erect in her hand. Todd had never felt anything so glorious. He reached tentatively for her, and she grabbed his hand with her free one and stuffed it inside her dress. Her full, smooth breast filled his hand and he was in heaven.

"Now this just doesn't look like a good idea to me," Clint said.

Both Annabelle and Todd pulled back from each other, Todd quickly stuffing himself back into his pants.

"What are you doing here?" Annabelle demanded. "Did my husband send you?"

"Nobody sent me, Annabelle," Clint said. "I saw you leave your wagon."

"Why don't you mind your own business?" Todd demanded.

"This is my business, Todd."

"So what do you want?" Annabelle asked, getting to her feet. "You want me, too?"

"I want you to go back to your wagon, Annabelle."

"No, you don't," she said, undoing the front of her dress.

"Annabelle—" Todd said.

"You want me," she said, drawing her breasts out of her dress. Clint had to admit they were beautiful breasts, full and smooth and pale in the moonlight. She held them in her hands and squeezed them.

"I can handle both of you," she said to Clint, "the legend and the boy. I'm enough woman for both of you."

"Annabelle," Todd said, shocked, "what're you sayin'?"

"She's not the girl you thought she was, Todd, is she?"

Annabelle's eyes were unfocused, and Clint wasn't even sure she could hear what he was saying. He stepped forward, grabbed her dress and pulled it closed, then pushed her away from him.

"Go back to your wagon, Annabelle," he said. "Back to your husband."

"He's not my husband," she said. "He's my brother, and I'm tired of fucking him. I wanna fuck somebody else for a change."

"Annabelle—" Todd said, in a whisper.

"She's sick, Todd," Clint said, "she's a sick girl. Get your things. We're leaving right now."

"You can't leave," Annabelle said. Then: "Yes! Yes you can, and take me with you."

"Todd," Clint said, "get the horses. Come on, Annabelle."

Clint took her by the arm and pulled her back to camp.

"I don't know what's between you and Judd, Annabelle," Clint said, "and I don't want to know. Just go back to your wagon and we'll be on our way."

"Judd!" she shouted. "Judd! They're leavin'!"

Judd came charging out of the wagon, and there was something new. He was wearing a gun on his hip.

"What's going on?"

"They're pullin' out now."

"Time for Todd and I to go, Judd. I don't know what's going on between you and your wife, or your sister, or whatever—"

"You told them?" Judd demanded. "You told them you're my sister?"

"Yes!" Annabelle said. "I want to get away from you."

"Annabelle, you bitch—"

Judd drew his gun and fired at Annabelle before Clint or Todd could do anything. It caught Clint by surprise, and that angered him. He never expected the man to draw and fire at a woman.

The bullet hit Annabelle in the chest. Blood blossomed on her dress and she fell onto her back.

"Annabelle?" Judd asked. Suddenly, he seemed remorseful for what he'd done. "Annabelle? Get up, Annabelle."

He holstered his gun and rushed to her, took her in her arms.

"Annabelle, wake up."

Todd came up behind Clint with the horses, both saddled and ready to go.

"Get my bedroll and saddlebags," Clint told him.

"Is she dead?" the boy asked.

"She's dead, Todd," Clint said. "Go on, do what I tell you."

Clint looked down at Judd, who was crying over his sister now. What had happened to these two, he wondered, to make them as sick as they were?

"Judd," Clint said, "come on, Judd."

"You!" Judd said, looking up at Clint. "This is because you came here."

Clint couldn't help but think Judd was right. This had happened because he and Todd came into camp, but it might have happened with anybody.

"Judd, listen—"

Judd dropped his sister's body to the ground and stood, his hand hovering near his gun. When he drew and fired at Annabelle it had been fast, about as fast as Clint had ever seen.

"Judd, don't—"

"Your fault," Judd said. "I'll kill you."

The younger man drew and he was fast, but not fast enough. Clint drew and fired, hitting Judd in the chest. The man coughed, staggered and then fell across his sister's body.

Todd came up behind Clint again and stared down at the two dead people.

"What happened here, Clint?" he asked. "What the hell happened here?"

"Let's get away from here, Todd," Clint said. "We may never figure it out, but we're sure as hell not going to figure it out here."

TWENTY-FOUR

They rode through the night and didn't stop until first light. They didn't talk either until they had dismounted and each picked out a rock to sit on.

"What happened back there?" Todd asked again.

"I don't know, Todd," Clint said. "I do know I made a big mistake taking us into that camp."

"B-but . . . what kind of people were they?"

"Sick people," Clint said. "They didn't seem that way, but they were."

"H-he killed her."

"And I had to kill him," Clint said, "and we had to leave them there. What we should have done was bury them, but . . ."

"I just wanted to get away from there as fast as I could," Todd said.

Clint looked at him and said, "So did I, son. So did I. But that's no excuse for not burying them. We'll just have to live with that, I guess."

"But—but she was so nice."

"She was playing with you, Todd," Clint said. "I told you that."

"But how was I supposed to know?"

"You weren't," Clint said, "but you are supposed to learn from this."

Todd thought a moment, then shook his head.

"I guess I was kind of stupid thinking she'd be interested in a sixteen-year-old kid."

"You weren't thinking with your head, Todd."

"Right," the boy said. "I was using my heart."

Clint slapped the boy on the shoulder and said, "You weren't thinking with that, either."

Todd looked at Clint, and then blushed.

"You've got plenty of time ahead of you for that, Todd."

"No," Todd said, "this convinces me. I just have to go ahead and do what I got to do and not worry about anything else."

"Just learn something from this experience, son," Clint said, "so it doesn't go to waste."

"I learned—what kind of people were they? I mean . . . do you really think they were brother and sister?"

"I can't answer that, Todd," Clint said. "I can't answer any part of that question. You just have to file this away under 'things aren't always what they seem to be,' and move on."

"I suppose you're right," Todd said. "I mean, I know you're right. You told me, I should have listened."

This time Clint simply placed his hand on the boy's shoulder and said, "Someday I'll remind you that you just said that."

TWENTY-FIVE

Clint had never been to Dirtville. He had only heard about it. His information was that this was the nearest town to Dead Horse Canyon. That still left a lot of leeway as to where Dead Horse Canyon was.

"Who ever named this town Dortville?" Todd wondered aloud. "I like Dirtville a lot better."

"So do a lot of people."

"How did you hear about this place?"

"I know certain people who some folks would think of as bad men," Clint said. "They talk about this place. It's up there with the Hole in the Wall Gang, and the Devil's Hole Gang as a sort of legendary place for outlaws."

"Don't you know anybody who could just . . . tell you where it is?" Todd asked him.

"I don't think anyone would just tell me, Todd," Clint said. "That would be breaking some sort of code. Somebody might give me a hint, though. That's why we're going to send out some telegrams."

Also, with this being the closest town to the canyon maybe someone would hear about it when they did send some telegrams. Also, someone from the canyon might actually come into town. After all, they needed supplies there.

Todd had been somewhat easier to talk to since the incident with Judd and Annabelle. He seemed very contrite and embarrassed by the whole thing, and eager to make up for it.

They rode to the livery where they left their horses and took their gear to one of Dirtville's two hotels.

"Maybe we should start asking around?" Todd said, in a low voice as they entered the hotel.

"Not quite yet, Todd," Clint said. "Let's wait a while before we do that. Just let me do the talking, all right?"

"Sure," Todd said. "You're the boss."

Clint only hoped that Todd would keep that attitude, for a while.

Clint got two rooms, as the hotel was far from full. Dirtville was smaller than Blissful had been, but Blissful had looked busier, more alive. Dirtville just seemed to . . . sit there.

They went to their rooms and Clint looked down from his window at the main street. There was a knock as his door and he opened it to admit Todd.

"How's your room?"

"I ain't never had my own hotel room before," Todd said.

"Do you like it?"

"Yeah, I do."

"Bed okay?"

"Better than what I ever had at home."

The beds were little more than pallets, so Clint could only imagine what Todd had been sleeping on at home.

"What do we do now?" Todd asked.

"Several things," Clint said. "First, we get a meal, then we take a look around town. Third, I check in with the local sheriff."

"Why? Will he know where Dead Horse Canyon is?"

"He might," Clint said, "but I'm not going to ask him."

"Then why talk to him?"

"Because someone in town might recognize me and then he'd come looking for me. This way I introduce myself to him, tell him I'll be in town a few days and he won't worry about it."

"Do you do that all the time?" Todd asked. "Introduce yourself to the sheriff when you get to a town?"

"Most of the time," Clint said. "Especially if I'm going to be spending some time there."

"What do I do while you're talking to the sheriff?"

"Stay in your room," Clint said. "But first, let's go get that meal."

"I hope someplace in this town has good food," Todd said. "That stew Annabelle made . . ." Todd trailed off.

"I know," Clint said. "She was a fine cook."

And beautiful, Todd thought, and she smelled good and tasted good, and felt good . . . God, her hands on him had felt so good . . . would any woman's hands feel that good, he wondered?

Did Dirtville have a whorehouse?

He'd never thought about being with a whore before . . . well, he had thought of it once or twice while living at home, but he hadn't thought about it recently. Since Annabelle, though, he'd been thinking about it a lot. He wondered if Clint would take him, if he asked.

They left the hotel and went looking for a place to eat.

Ed Cahill was the one who always made the trip from Dead Horse Canyon to Dirtville with a buckboard to collect supplies. He usually checked in with the telegraph office, too, to see if Atkins or Gilette had gotten any telegrams from anyone.

Cahill was loading supplies into the buckboard when

he saw the man and the boy come out of the hotel across the street. He'd never seen either of them before, and yet they both looked familiar. Gilette told him to always be on the lookout for strangers when he went to town, and these two were certainly strangers.

He waited for the man and boy to pick a direction and wander off in it, then he brushed off his hands and started across the street. A quick look at the register in the hotel might answer a lot of questions.

TWENTY-SIX

Clint knew they had no hope of finding a place in town where the food would be as good as Annabelle's stew, but they did find a place that could make a steak dinner that was edible.

"Not as good as that stew," Todd announced when they were finished eating, "but better than what I got at home."

"I take it your mother was not a very good cook."

"No," Todd said, "she was awful—but I never told her that."

"You were a good son."

"Yeah," Todd said, "yeah, I was. I had to make up for the fact that Pa wasn't there. And now I got to—" He stopped short and said, instead, "I wonder how the pie is here?"

"Only one way to find out," Clint said.

It, too, was edible.

When they left the café they took a walk around town. It didn't take long, because Dirtville was not very big. During their walk they passed the sheriff's office.

"Well," Clint said, "at least they've got an office. You

better go back to the hotel and I'll see if they have a sheriff, too."

"What can I do in my room?" Todd complained.

"Try cleaning your rifle," Clint said. "It needs it after all those nights on a dusty trail."

"What about your guns?"

"I'll be cleaning them tonight, too," Clint said. "I always keep my guns clean, Todd. It's how I stay alive."

"Okay, okay," Todd said, "I get your point. I'll clean my rifle and wait for you in my room."

"Thank you."

They split up, Clint crossing the street to the sheriff's office and Todd walking to the hotel. Clint paused in front of the sheriff's office long enough to make sure that was where Todd was going, and then he turned the doorknob and entered.

A man was standing at a potbellied stove—a staple of the Western sheriff's office—pouring himself a cup of coffee. He turned at the sound of his door opening. He was a sad-faced man in his forties, who might have been sad because he was in his forties and the sheriff of a town people called Dirtville.

"Can I help ya?" he asked.

"Sheriff," Clint said, "my name is Clint Adams."

The sheriff put his coffee pot down with a bang.

"The Gunsmith?"

"That's right."

"Well . . . what brings you to Dirtville?"

"I'm just passing through," Clint said, "and thought I'd let you know I was here. I'm traveling with a youngster who's looking for his father. I'm trying to help him find him."

"In Dirtville?"

"Not necessarily," Clint said. "We're just stopping here to rest for a few days."

"Well, I appreciate you comin' in and lettin' me know you're here. I just hope you'll be able to stay out of— uh, I mean, avoid trouble."

"I always try to do that," Clint said. "Do you get much trouble around here?"

The sheriff narrowed his eyes and stared at Clint. The people of Dirtville must have known how close they were to the legendary Dead Horse Canyon. Certainly, the local sheriff must have known.

"It's a small town," the lawman finally said. "That means whatever trouble we have is usually small."

"Well, that's good," Clint said. "I'll do my best to stay out of your hair, sheriff. We're just looking to relax for a few days, let our animals rest a bit."

"Just let me know when you're gettin' ready to leave," the sheriff said.

"What's your name, sheriff?"

"Marbury," the man said, "Steve Marbury. Been sheriff here for about five years or so."

"Guess you must know the area pretty well."

Again, the man narrowed his eyes as he stared at Clint.

"Somethin' in particular you're lookin' for?"

"Nope," Clint said, "nothin'. Just makin' conversation."

The sheriff took his cup of coffee around behind his desk with him and sat down, then looked up at Clint.

"So you've heard the stories, have you?"

"About what?"

"Dead Horse Canyon?"

"Dead Horse Canyon is a myth," Clint said. "It doesn't exist."

"That's right, it doesn't," Marbury said. "So it wouldn't make any sense for you to be here lookin' for it, would it?"

"No, sir, it sure wouldn't," Clint said.

"Well, that's good," Marbury said. "I figured a man as smart as you are wouldn't be caught up in that nonsense."

"No, I'm sure not," Clint said. "Well, it was good to meet you, sheriff."

"Same here, Mr. Adams," Marbury said, "same here."

Clint went to the door and left, stopping just outside to give his visit some thought. They'd played word game for a while before the sheriff finally was the one to mention Dead Horse Canyon. He certainly knew about it, but just how much did he actually know?

That was the question.

TWENTY-SEVEN

After Clint Adams left the sheriff's office, Ed Cahill stepped from the doorway he'd been standing in across the street, crossed over and entered the sheriff's office.

"Do you know who that was?" he asked the sheriff.

"I do."

"Clint Adams."

"I know."

"I checked at the hotel," Cahill said. "He registered as Clint Adams."

"He's not tryin' to hide," Marbury said. "He introduced himself to me."

"I saw him once, and I thought he looked familiar when I saw him today," Cahill said. "When I saw his name on the register I knew it was him."

"Ed," Sheriff Marbury said, "he came in here and introduced himself. He's Clint Adams."

"I know!" Cahill said. "What's he doin' here?"

"Says he's just passin' through."

"He's got a kid with him," Cahill said, "a boy about sixteen or seventeen. What's that about?"

"He says he's trying to help the boy find his father."

"He's lookin' for Dead Horse Canyon, that's what he's doin'," Cahill said.

"Why would Clint Adams want the canyon?" Cahill said. "He's no outlaw, and he ain't a lawman."

"Maybe you shoulda asked him."

"I mentioned it."

"What did he say?"

"He said Dead Horse Canyon is a myth."

"What's that?"

"It means it doesn't exist," Marbury said, "that it's not real."

"Look," Cahill said, "he's the goddamned Gunsmith. He should know if it exists or not. He's got enough friends on both sides of the law."

"What are you worried about?" Marbury asked. "You think he's comin' after you?"

"I just got to know what to tell Gilette and Trace, that's all."

"Tell them that Clint Adams is in town, and that I had a talk with him. Tell them he says he's just passin' through. Tell them I got no reason to doubt that he's tellin' the truth. Tell 'em all that."

"Yeah," Cahill said, "yeah, okay."

"And get out of town before Adams starts wonderin' about you the way you're wonderin' about him."

"Yeah, okay," Cahill said. "I'm goin'. I got to bring the supplies back, anyway."

"Good," Marbury said. "Adams says he's gonna stay out of trouble, and that's the way I want it. You better tell Atkins to keep the boys in the canyon, don't let them come into town. One of them is bound to want to try the Gunsmith on for size."

"You're right about that."

"And Ed."

"Yeah?" Cahill stopped right in front of the door.

"Tell Atkins and Gilette about him," Marbury said,

"but don't tell anyone else. Like Adams said, we don't want no trouble while he's here."

"Okay," Cahill said, "yeah, okay."

Cahill left and Marbury cursed. Why did Cahill have to come in for supplies today? If there was one thing Ed Cahill would never be able to do, it was keep his mouth shut about Clint Adams being in town. Some hotshot in the canyon was going to come looking for Adams, for sure.

Trouble was right around the corner.

TWENTY-EIGHT

"What'd the sheriff say about Dead Horse Canyon?" Todd asked when Clint got back to the hotel.

"We both agreed it was a myth."

"Why?"

"Because I don't want him to know we're looking for it."

"Why not?"

"Because we don't know who he'll tell."

"Oh, I get it," Todd said. "He might tell somebody from Dead Horse Canyon."

"Right."

"But if you send telegrams—"

"They might find out anyway," Clint finished. "But they'll find out when I'm ready for them to."

"And when will that be?"

"Let's give it a day," Clint said. "Tomorrow is soon enough. Meanwhile, let's see what happens. The sheriff might mention it to someone, anyway."

"You mean someone might come after us tonight?"

"It's possible."

"What do we do if they do?"

"We stay alive long enough to tell them who you are,"

Clint said. "Then we'll find out if your father wants to see you."

"What if he doesn't?"

"We'll have to take it one step at a time, Todd," Clint said. "One step at a time."

Ed Cahill drove the supply buckboard into Dead Horse Canyon at breakneck speed. He didn't even stop to exchange pleasantries with the men who were on guard, which was his usual pattern.

As he reined the team in at the center of the canyon men came out to see what all the commotion was.

"Clint Adams!" Cahill shouted, dropping down from the seat of the buckboard. "Clint Adams is in Dirtville!"

"Who?" someone asked.

"The Gunsmith!" Cahill said. "He's in Dirtville."

Gilette and Atkins came out of Atkins's house, where they were sitting having coffee.

"Get that idiot in here," Atkins said to Gilette.

"Right."

"And don't let anyone leave the canyon until we find out what the hell is going on."

"Okay."

Atkins went back inside and Gilette went up to Cahill. The man opened his mouth to say something but Gilette grabbed him by the throat.

"Shut the hell up and get inside," he said.

He pushed Cahill toward the house and released him.

"Did you hear him?" Will Tayback said to Gilette. "The goddamned Gunsmith is in Dirtville."

"So?" Gilette asked.

"This is somebody's chance to make a name for themselves," Tayback said.

"You, Will?" Gilette asked. "You want to take on the Gunsmith with a gun, one on one?"

"Not me, Ed," Tayback said. "I was thinkin' of you."

"Nobody leaves the canyon, Will," Gilette said. "Got that? Nobody."

"But Ed—"

"Not unless you hear it from Trace."

"Or from you."

"Yeah," Gilette said, "or from me. Pass the word."

"Okay, Ed," Tayback said. "Okay."

Gilette turned and walked back to the house. If Clint Adams truly was in Dirtville, then it had to have something to do with Dead Horse Canyon. What other reason would there be for such a man to be around?

TWENTY-NINE

Trace Atkins listened to what Cahill had to say, with Eddie Gilette standing in a corner with his arms crossed. Belinda was across the room, at the stove, preparing some coffee. It was quite a little domestic scene, Gilette thought, but now wasn't the time to say anything about it.

"And the sheriff said he's not looking for the canyon?" Atkins asked.

"That's right, Trace," Cahill said. "But what other reason could he have for being in town?"

"He could be passing through," Gilette said. "Like he says."

"Could be," Atkins said, stroking his chin. "But maybe somebody should check it out, Eddie."

Cahill was "Ed" and Gilette was "Eddie," although Gilette always referred to Cahill simply by his last name.

"What about the boy?" Cahill asked.

"What about him?" Atkins asked.

"The sheriff said he's tryin' to help the boy find his father," Cahill said. "Anybody here got a son someplace?"

Atkins looked at Gilette, but didn't say anything.

"We can check with the men," he said, instead, "and see who's got kids out there, somewhere."

"Meanwhile," Gilette said, "with Cahill running his big mouth outside a lot of the men want to go to town to get a look at the Gunsmith."

"We can't have that," Atkins said, scratching his head. "That'd just be looking for trouble."

"You'll have to talk to them, Trace," Gilette said.

"Okay," Atkins said, "but somebody's got to go to town and check on the Gunsmith, Eddie. It's got to be somebody we can trust to stay out of trouble, though. We got anybody here like that?"

Gilette gave Atkins a baleful stare, knowing what the man was leading up to.

"We got a bunch of hotheads here, Trace," he said. "You know that as well as I do."

"Well," Atkins said, "I guess that leaves it up to you or me, doesn't it?"

"If you go, you can't go alone," Cahill said to Atkins. "You're the boss."

"I guess that leaves you, Eddie," Atkins said, looking at Gilette.

"Tomorrow," Gilette said, "I'll take a ride into town tomorrow and see what's goin' on. For now, though, you better go out there and talk to the men."

"I will," Atkins said. "Come on, Cahill. Let's see if we can undo the damage you've done with your big mouth."

Cahill got up and whined, "Aw, I didn't mean nothin' by it. I was just excited . . ."

His voice trailed off as he and Atkins went out the door, leaving Gilette and Belinda alone.

"Coffee, Eddie?" she asked.

"Sure."

He walked to the table and sat down. He was thinking

about his son, Todd. How old would he be now? And would he be out here looking for his father?

Belinda brought him a cup of coffee and stood next to him, looking down.

"You've got a son somewhere, don't you, Eddie?"

"Kentucky."

"How old is he?"

"I lost track."

Fifteen, sixteen, maybe, Gilette was thinking. Since the boy's birth he'd gone back and forth to Kentucky to see him and his mother, but years ago he and the mother had had a real big fight and he left. That was the last he'd ever seen of mother or son. Come to think of it, he and Trace and the rest of the men—some of the same group that was with them today—had taken the town with them . . . at least, everything of value in the town. Gilette's temper had gotten the better of him that day, and he'd convinced Atkins to clean out that town. Later, he realized what kind of position that must have left the woman and the boy in, but it was too late to do anything about it, then.

Would the boy grow up hating him after that? Would that hate lead him to come looking for him? And had he ever mentioned Dead Horse Canyon to the woman or the boy?

"Come on, Eddie," Belinda said, "you know how old your own boy would be."

"Forget it, Belinda," he said. "There'd be no reason for any son of mine to come lookin' for me."

"Sorry," she said, with a shrug. "Just makin' conversation." She waked back to the stove.

"What are you doin', anyway?" Gilette asked.

"What do you mean?"

"I mean makin' coffee, cookin'," Gilette said. "That's not why you're here, Belinda."

"Trace likes when I cook—"

"You and the other women, you're here for all the men," Gilette said. "Not just for Trace."

"Trace likes me to—"

"You're ruinin' him, Belinda," Gilette said, standing up.

"What?"

"Ruinin' him as the leader here," Gilette said. "You're makin' him break the rules he's supposed to be enforcing."

"Trace does what he wants—"

"No," Gilette said, "I think Trace has been doin' what you want him to do, and I'm wonderin' how much further you and he are gonna take this?"

"I think you'd have to take that up with Trace, Eddie," Belinda said, "if you dare."

At that point Atkins came back into the house and saw Gilette and Belinda glaring at each other.

"What's goin' on?" he asked.

"Nothin'," Gilette said, heading for the door, "nothin' at all."

"What was that all about?" Atkins asked Belinda after Gilette had left.

"I think he's worried that the boy in town might be his, come looking for him," Belinda said.

"That's why he's going to town tomorrow," Atkins said. "To deal with it. What else is goin' on?"

"He doesn't approve of us," Belinda said.

"It doesn't matter whether he approves or not," Atkins said. "I'm still the leader here."

"Let him be the leader."

"What?"

"Let's leave and let him be the leader," she said. "Why

hasn't he ever been the leader? He's been here the longest."

"He doesn't want to be."

"Then let them pick someone else after we've gone," Belinda said. "Look, with the Gunsmith in the area this is a good time for us to leave."

"I never said I'd leave, Belinda."

She approached him, put her arms around his waist and pressed her head to his chest. He was her man, and she wasn't going to let any gang keep him from her.

"Do you love me, Trace?"

"You know I do." He put his arms around her as well.

"Then we have to leave," she said. "You know that."

"We will," he said, patting her shoulder, "we will leave, Belinda . . . just not quite yet."

THIRTY

Clint and Todd took one more walk around town before returning to the hotel for Todd to turn in. Clint wanted Todd to see if he recognized any of the faces he saw as gang members.

"That was years ago, Clint," Todd said. "Plenty of members have probably come and gone since then."

"Maybe your father, too."

"Maybe."

They reached the hotel and stopped in front of it.

"You better go up to bed and get some rest."

"What about you?" Todd asked.

"I'm going to go over to the saloon, see what I can find out."

"You gonna ask about Dead Horse Canyon?" Todd asked.

"No," Clint said, "I'm just going to stand around and listen. Sometimes you can find out more that way. Go on, I'll see you in the morning."

Clint waited for Todd to go inside, then turned and walked toward the saloon.

• • •

Joe wanted to go into town.

"Why do we have to stay camped out here?" he demanded.

"It's a small town, Joe," Lem said. "Adams would see us right away."

"So what? We got just as much right to be there as he does."

"We'll just wait here for the rest to catch up to us."

They had arranged for three men to join them, all men they both knew from their past, men they had worked with before. None of the three, however, had ever been to Dead Horse Canyon. In fact, Lem and Joe had never been there, they just had friends who had. They both knew a man named Will Tayback, who was part of the Atkins gang, but Tayback had never told them where the canyon was.

"Don't see why we can't sneak into town in the dark, find a place to stay . . ." Joe muttered, poking at the campfire with a stick, causing it to flare up.

"Stop playin' with the fire, damn it!"

Joe dropped the stick into the fire.

"Turn in, will you?" Lem said. "The others will catch up with us tomorrow. We'll go into town then, not before."

"Fine," Joe said, "but I wanna be the first one to put a bullet in the Gunsmith. I want to make him pay for makin' me sleep on the ground tonight."

"Fine," Lem said, "you put the first bullet in him," and then added to himself, "if he doesn't put one in you first."

Gilette went to his cabin and closed the door, locking it securely. It was only in here that he ever felt comfortable enough to remove his gun, and his boots, and relax. He had boarded up the windows a long time ago so no one could see in. He hadn't even left gunports in the wooden shutters. This was his safe haven.

He went to the stove and put on a pot of coffee. It was all he ever used the stove for, besides heat. When he ate he ate outside with the men. That was something Atkins used to do, too, until recently, when he'd taken to eating in his cabin with Belinda. A lot of the men had noticed this, and mentioned it to Gilette. He'd told them to mind their own business, he'd take care of it.

Atkins wasn't listening to him, though. He still acted like he forgot who had made him the leader. He acted like he could do anything he wanted to do, including breaking long-standing canyon rules. But that wasn't the case at all.

Gilette took his coffee to the table and sat. The only furniture he had was this table, two chairs, and a bed against the wall. It was a real bed, with a real mattress, that he'd had brought in years ago. It was the only concession to comfort in the whole canyon. It was also the reason most of the women wanted to spend the night with him, so they'd get to sleep in his bed. Lately, however, he had not been bringing many of the women in here.

He thought about going into town tomorrow. It didn't bother him that he might run into the Gunsmith. That would just be interesting. But the boy . . . what if it *was* his son? What if it *was* Todd? What could he say to him? Could the boy be coming here to join him? Wouldn't that be something, to have his own son in the gang with him? Maybe that would be the time to take on the role of leader? If he was the boss, maybe he could train his son to be the one to take over, maybe in four or five years?

Wouldn't that be something?

But what if the boy had come looking for him, just to tell him he hated him? Or worse? And how the hell had the boy gotten himself hooked up with the Gunsmith?

Then again, maybe it wasn't his boy. He'd just go into town tomorrow and find out, that's all. One look at the boy and . . . Jesus, would he even recognize the boy after three or four years? How different would a sixteen-year-old look from the twelve-year-old he'd seen last?

He'd lied to Belinda about not knowing Todd's age. He remembered. He even remembered the day the boy was born, and he remembered the day he left the boy and his mother.

He tried to forget everything that had happened in between.

Todd sat in his room, wondering if he should stay there or get out. He'd never had his own hotel room before, but he wasn't in Dirtville to find comfort; he was there to find his father. Find him and kill him. He still wasn't going to be able to do that without Clint, though, so for just a little while longer he'd do as he was told.

He was close, though. He knew he was closer than ever to fulfilling the promise he'd made to his mother.

THIRTY-ONE

Clint claimed a spot at the bar in the saloon and nursed a beer, eavesdropping on conversations taking place around him. There was a small poker game going on in one corner, but he decided to stay away from it for the time being. Later, however, he was able to determine that the game was between a group of regulars—except that there was one empty chair. He'd found out nothing from eavesdropping, so now he was considering the game a possible source of information.

"Always an empty chair in that game?" he asked the bartender.

"Naw," the man said. "There's usually six players but Clem couldn't make it tonight."

"What's wrong with Clem?"

"Wife had a baby," the man said.

"And that interferes with poker?"

The bartender smiled and said, "What're ya gonna do?"

"Think they'd let me sit in?"

"You could ask," the barkeep said, 'but it's a small game. Mostly just a way to pass the time."

"That's all I'm looking to do."

"Can't hurt to ask, then."

Clint finished his beer and set the empty mug down.

"Another?"

Clint shook his head.

"I never drink when I play poker."

"That puts you ahead of most of those boys already."

Clint walked across the room and stopped by the empty chair.

"You boys mind a stranger sitting in?" he asked.

All five men looked up at him, and then four of them looked at the fifth man. He was in his fifties, wearing a white shirt with long sleeves rolled up and a black jacket draped over the back of the chair. He was, apparently, the man in charge of the game.

"Just ride in?" the man asked.

"Today," Clint said.

"Passin' through?"

"Yep," Clint said. "I'm just looking for a way to pass the time tonight."

"Well," the man said, "it's a regular game, and a small one. Just so happens one of our players couldn't play tonight. Five card stud okay with you? It's all we play."

"That's fine."

"Nickels and dimes," the man said, "that's all we play for, nickel and dimes."

"That's fine, too."

"Pull up a chair, then," the man said. "Hope you got some change, 'cause he don't have no chips."

"I can make some change at the bar," Clint said. "Be right back."

He went back to the bar and asked for some change.

"Looks like you're in," the bartender said.

"Looks like. Who's the fella who did the talking?"

"That's Doc."

"Just Doc?"

"His name's Doc Page," the bartender said.

"That his name, or is he really the doctor?"

"He's really the doctor."

"Wait a minute," Clint said. "Clem couldn't come because his wife had a baby, but her doctor's here?"

"Why not?" the bartender asked. "He delivered it already."

Clint accepted his change and said, "That's true."

He went back to the table with his change and occupied the empty chair.

"You can get the name of everyone as we go along," Doc Page said.

"Names aren't as important as cards," Clint said.

"Boys," one of the other players said, "I think we might just be in some trouble here."

It was clearly a game of regulars passing the time because none of the players except for Doc Page exhibited any real understanding of the game. In fact, Clint was fairly sure that Doc used this game to fleece the other players out of their money.

He wondered if any of these players had come in from Dead Horse Canyon, then decided not. The conversation seemed to center around things that were happening in town, which led Clint to believe that they were all living in town.

He played carelessly because he wanted to listen in on the conversation, but when he realized that he wasn't going to find out anything useful, he began to pay more attention to the game.

He also noticed that while the other men talked Doc remained silent and concentrated on his cards. One of the players even stayed in the game when it was clear—to Doc and Clint, anyway—that his cards were either on the table or had already been folded by one of the other players.

After the first hour Clint began concentrating more on his hand, and on Doc Page's.

During one hand in particular Clint called Doc on a big bet—big for this game—and it turned out that Doc was bluffing.

"Whoa," one of the other players said. "I don't think I ever saw Doc called on a bluff before."

"Just got lucky," Clint said, raking the pot in, but he was drawing a hard look from Doc Page, across the table from him.

"My deal . . ." Clint said, gathering up the cards.

At the end of the second hour it was clear that Clint was outplaying Doc. Even the other players, who were still losing, noticed it, and the more they mentioned it the madder Doc got.

"Whatsa matter, Doc?" one of them asked. "Don't like havin' some competition for a change?" He looked at Clint and said, "Mister, we ain't even seen anybody beat ol' Doc before."

"Like I said before," Clint said, "I'm just sort of lucky."

"Ain't luck, the way you been playing," Doc said, quietly.

"What?" Clint asked.

"I said what you've been doing ain't luck."

"What is it then, Doc?" one of the other players asked.

"Yeah," another man said, "what are ya sayin', Doc?"

They were all wondering if Doc was about to accuse Clint of cheating, and Clint was wondering the same thing. He was wondering how he should react to being called a cheat in a nickel and dime game like this.

"All I'm saying," Doc said, "is that the man knows

how to play poker. He ain't lucky; he's good."

Everybody at the table relaxed and smiled, and Clint was also relieved. He also thought that maybe he should lose some of the money back to Doc and then turn in before something went wrong.

"A few more hands, gents," he said, "and then I'm off to bed."

"Gotta give me a chance to win my money back," Doc Page said.

Clint smiled and said, "That's why I said a few more hands, Doc. Shouldn't take a good player like you more than that to recoup his losses."

"I didn't say I was losing," Doc replied, "but you do have some of my money in front of you."

"Hell," another player said, "he's got lots of our money in front of him, Doc. The man wants to go to sleep I say let 'im."

"I'll stay a while," Clint said. "Is it my deal?"

Clint had to lose some of the money back to Doc without making it obvious he was doing so. He didn't think the doctor would be very happy with that turn of events, either.

He managed to catch Doc bluffing one more time, but he let the physician catch him two or three times, as well. By the time he was ready to leave the game Doc had gotten most of his money back from Clint, who was still a little ahead. Doc also had a lot of money that formerly belonged to the other players. Clint thought it was time to call it a night.

"Well, thanks for letting me into the game, gentlemen," he said, picking up his money and standing up.

"Quitting already?" Doc asked.

"Long day," Clint said, "and another one ahead of me. Maybe another time?"

"Here every night," Doc said. "If you're still around tomorrow, be glad to have you."

"Thanks, Doc," Clint said. "I appreciate that."

Clint left the saloon, no wiser when it came to Dead Horse Canyon, but determined to find another way to pass the time other than sitting in on a "friendly little game." If Doc wanted to fleece his neighbors, that was his business, and if they wanted to let him—well, that was also theirs.

THIRTY-TWO

Clint walked past Todd's room on the way back to his own. He didn't intend to wake him, but before he could enter his room Todd's door opened and the boy stepped out.

"I couldn't sleep and thought I heard you walking by," he said. "Did you find out anything?"

"Yeah," Clint said, "I found out that I shouldn't sit in on another man's game."

"What?"

"Never mind," Clint said. "I didn't find out anything helpful about Dead Horse Canyon. You might as well just go to bed and we'll see what we can find out about it tomorrow."

"All right," Todd said, "but I don't think I'll be able to sleep."

"You'd be surprised. Good night."

"Good night."

They both went into their rooms, and each was asleep moments after their heads hit the pillows.

Eddie Gilette rose early that morning and was, as usual, the first one out for coffee and breakfast. Starling handed him his first cup and then stood there, staring at him.

"What?" Gilette asked.

"Don't you think it's time, Eddie?"

"Time for what?"

"For you to step up and take over," Starling said. "For you to put a stop to this changing line of leaders in this gang."

"The leaders aren't the only thing that changes, Starling," Gilette said. "The gang itself changes."

"You can put a stop to that, too. When you made me leader, Eddie, I knew it. Atkins, he doesn't know it—not anymore."

"Why'd you stay?" Gilette asked. "When Trace took over, why'd you stay and become . . . this."

"Because this," Starling said, spreading his hands to indicate himself, "is all I had left. Don't let this happen to you, Eddie. The longer you wait, the more chance there is that it will."

Gilette finished his coffee and handed the cup back to Starling.

"I'll keep that in mind."

"Another cup?"

"No," Gilette said, "I got to go into town."

"What about breakfast?"

"I'll get somethin' there."

Starling watched as Gilette walked over to where the horses were and he said, "Good luck" to the man's retreating back.

Clint woke with the early morning light in his eyes. He rolled over to get away from it, but the lumps in the mattress would not let him get comfortable again. He got out of bed, poured some water in the basin from the pitcher on the dresser and washed his face and torso before dressing. He walked to the window and looked out.

There wasn't a soul on the streets of Dirtville, and then suddenly a lone rider appeared. He rode down the main street slowly, never looking to his right or his left. Then, suddenly, he looked up, directly at Clint's window. It was as if the two men actually locked eyes, but the rider kept going, never paused, never altered his pace.

It was enough, though, for Clint. He had seen the rider's face clearly and that one look was all he needed to tell him that this was Eddie Gilette.

This was Todd's father.

There would be no need for telegrams, or anymore eavesdropping. If Gilette was in town, then Dead Horse Canyon was very near. But with the man's presence in town, maybe that didn't much matter anymore, either. Todd didn't want to find Dead Horse Canyon so much as he wanted to find his father.

Clint left the window and went down to the lobby. He walked past Todd's door and it never even occurred to him to wake the boy up.

Gilette took his horse to the livery. He didn't know how long he'd be in town, but he didn't want to leave the horse on the street.

"Just keep him ready," he told the liveryman.

"Right, Mr. Gilette."

Gilette left his saddlebags and rifle at the livery and started walking back toward the center of town.

Clint stepped out of the hotel and looked both ways. Eddie Gilette was nowhere in sight. The man must have ridden to the end of the street, or else he had gone all the way to the livery.

Coincidence that he had ridden into town this morning? Probably not. It was more likely the sheriff had sent a message to Dead Horse Canyon, or someone had recognized Clint—and maybe even the boy—and taken the information back to the canyon. Who better to come into town and check it out than Gilette himself?

Clint was about to step into the street when he saw Gilette walking toward him from the far end of town. He was walking in the street, but eventually he stepped up onto the boardwalk on the same side as the hotel. All Clint had to do was stand still and the man would reach him, eventually.

Gilette saw the man standing out in front of the hotel. It was the same man he'd seen standing in the hotel window, he was sure. This had to be Clint Adams, the Gunsmith. It just felt right. This was the way it was supposed to happen, then, without the boy, at first.

Gilette was certain now that his son was in town. He had never been much of a father, but he thought it was a father's instinct that kicked in as he rode into town. He could "feel" the boy's presence.

Still, it would probably be better for him to talk with Clint Adams first, find out what the boy wanted . . . what Adams wanted . . .

Clint waited until Gilette came within five feet of him and stopped. He was wearing a gun on his right hip, and stood as if he knew how to use it.

"Buy you breakfast?" Clint asked.

"I could use a bite."

"Café down the street okay?"

"Good as any."

They walked down the street to the café together.

THIRTY-THREE

When Clint ordered steak and eggs Gilette went along with it. Sitting across from the outlaw Clint saw that the resemblance was even more uncanny. There was no doubt that Todd was Gilette's son.

"Is he here?" Gilette asked.

Clint nodded.

"He's at the hotel," he said. "He looks just like you."

"Does he?"

"It's amazing."

Gilette picked up his coffee cup and drank from it.

"He has a lot of questions," Clint said.

"I'll bet."

"So do you, I guess."

"Yeah."

"Go ahead, then," Clint said. "Ask."

"How did he end up with you?"

Clint told the story of the boy being arrested in Broken Branch for asking questions about Dead Horse Canyon.

"I have a big mouth," Gilette said. "I must have mentioned the place to his mother."

"He has a good memory."

"I guess the only other question I have is why he's here?"

133

"He wants to kill you."

Gilette didn't look surprised. The waiter came and put their breakfast plates down in front of them, then left.

"He wants you to do it?"

"No," Clint said, "he wants to do it himself. He says he promised his mother he would."

Gilette sat back.

"His mother wouldn't have asked him for that promise."

"I think he promised it to her," Clint said, "on her grave."

"Well," Gilette said, "that makes more sense."

"Maybe if you talked with him," Clint said, "apologized for leaving him and his mother—"

"How can I apologize for something like that?" Gilette asked. "Do you know what we did? We robbed the whole town, and then we left."

"I know," Clint said. "He told me. He told me he and his mother paid for that every day until she died—and then he left."

"How can I apologize to the boy for that?"

"Do you want to apologize?"

Gilette thought a moment, then said, "No. I did what I had to do, at the time. I can't apologize for that."

"Do you want your son to kill you?"

"No."

"Then you better think of something to tell him."

"You brought him here," Gilette said, "you get him out of here."

"I could do that," Clint said. "I could take him away from here, but I couldn't sit on him after that. He'd just come back on his own. One of your men would end up killing him, if not you, yourself."

"I wouldn't kill the boy," Gilette said. "Not my own son."

"But if he tried to get into Dead Horse Canyon some-body would kill him, wouldn't they?"

"Probably," Gilette said, "but then they'd have to deal with me."

"So it falls to you, Gilette," Clint said. "The boy is your son. Do something about this situation."

"What?"

"I don't know," Clint said. "It's your problem."

"Why are you here?' Gilette asked. "I mean specifically? What did Todd ask you to do?"

"He wants me to kill everyone else in the canyon," Clint said, "while he kills you."

"Did you tell him you'd do that?"

"I didn't tell I could, or would," Clint said. "My in-tention all along was to do what I'm doing now, talk to you. Try to get you to do something, or say something, that would change his mind."

Gilette thought a moment, chewing a piece of meat.

"I could ask him to join the gang," he said, after he swallowed.

"Perfect," Clint said. "That would make him an out-law. He'd become a killer soon enough, then, wouldn't he?"

"But not for killing his own father."

"What would Trace Atkins think of all this?"

"What do you know about Atkins?"

"I know that right now you're part of the Atkins gang."

"Well," Gilette said, "it may not be the Atkins gang for much longer. Trace has got his own problems right now."

"What kind?"

"Female."

"So again," Clint said, "this all falls to you. You've got to find some way to keep your son from killing you, and to keep him alive."

"I wouldn't know where to start," Gilette said. "I'm not exactly the world's greatest father."

"And you're not going to learn to be in the next few days," Clint said. "All you can do right now is meet with the boy and talk to him."

"Will you set that up?"

"I will. When?"

"As soon as possible," Gilette said. "Today, while I'm in town."

"I'll talk to him about it right after breakfast."

"Good," Gilette said. "I appreciate it."

"There's one thing you should be aware of, though."

"What's that?"

Clint pushed his plate away and leaned forward.

"If anything happens to that boy," Clint said, "I'm going to hold you personally responsible. Understand?"

"I understand real good," Gilette said. "Just you remember one thing."

"What's that?"

"You brought him here," Gilette said. "Without you he'd probably still be riding around aimlessly, no danger to me or himself. You brought him here, so you're the one who put him in the line of fire."

Clint stared at Gilette for a few moments, then sat back.

"You know," he said, "I can't argue with that."

"Just so we both know where we stand."

"I think we do."

"Fine," Gilette said. "Why don't you go and talk to the boy and I'll pay for breakfast."

"I was going to buy—"

"It's on me," Gilette said, waving Clint away. "Besides, I'll sit here a while longer, until you've talked with the boy."

"All right," Clint said, standing, "I'll come back here with his answer."

Gilette waved, and poured himself a cup of coffee as Clint went out the door.

THIRTY-FOUR

Todd was bleary-eyed when he answered the door to his room but his eyes cleared very quickly when Clint told him who he had just had breakfast with.

"Are you serious?"

Clint nodded.

"He's still over at the café."

Todd raced across the room to grab his rifle, then tried to run past Clint into the hall. Clint grabbed the rifle away from him, put his hand against the boy's bony, bare chest and pushed him so that he landed on the bed.

"What are ya doin'?" Todd demanded.

"Well, for one thing you're in your underwear," Clint said. "And for another the man wants to talk to you before you kill him."

"I don't want to talk to him!"

"Sure you do, Todd," Clint said. "Think about it. You've got questions before you kill him."

"Well," Todd said, grudgingly, "maybe I do."

"So get yourself dressed and I'll tell him that you're coming down to talk to him—and I'll keep this for now." Clint held Todd's rifle out.

"You'll give it back?"

"If you still want it after you've talked to him," Clint said, "I'll give it back."

"Okay," Todd said. "I'll get dressed and come down."

"I'll go and tell him."

"What—" Todd started, then stopped himself.

"What do you want to know?"

"What's he look like?"

"Like you, son," Clint said. "Just like you."

Clint found Gilette lingering over more coffee. He'd half expected the man to be gone. It takes a lot of nerve to stay and talk to the son you abandoned years before.

Clint walked over to the table and sat back down. Gilette looked at the rifle in his hand.

"Todd's," Clint said. "He tried to rush right over here and shoot you."

"Is he comin'?"

"He's on his way, to talk," Clint said.

"He might want his rifle back after we talk."

"I told him I'd give it back," Clint said.

"And will you?"

Clint shook his head. "I lied."

"Well," Gilette said, "we'll see what happens."

"I have a suggestion for you, Gilette."

"What's that?"

"What would you think about leaving the gang and riding off with your son?" Clint asked.

Gilette answered right away. "Wouldn't work."

"Why not?"

"Because I am who I am," Gilette said. "It's too late for me to change. If I did, it would make everything I've done in the past . . . worthless."

Clint wasn't sure he agreed with that, but then he wasn't sure he was in a position to argue it.

"All right," Clint said. "When Todd gets here I'll take a little walk—"

"No," Gilette said, "stay. I-I'd like you to stay."

"I'll ask Todd," Clint said. "If he wants me to go, I will."

"Fair enough."

"Why do you want me to stay?"

"The truth?"

"That would be nice."

"I'm scared."

"Well," Clint said, "I guess that's reason enough."

THIRTY-FIVE

Todd appeared at the door to the café, wiping his hands on his thighs. Clint didn't say anything, because the boy didn't immediately enter. He was trying to get his courage up.

Finally, when he walked in Clint said, "Here we go," and stood up.

Gilette stood up as well and turned to face the boy. The two looked at each other for a few moments without saying a word. Todd's eyes were wide and liquid, filled with anything but hate.

"Todd," Gilette said. "God, son, you've grown."

"Don't call me 'son,' " were Todd's first words to his father.

"All right," Gilette said. "I guess I had that comin'."

Todd looked at Clint.

"Todd, your father asked me to stay, but if you want me to go, I will," Clint told him.

"Naw, it's all right," Todd said. "You can stay. You came this far with me."

"Okay, fine."

Clint sat down and the other two men followed. The waiter came over and looked at Todd.

"I'll just have some coffee," he said. The waiter nodded, poured him a cup, and left.

"I guess we have a lot to talk about," Gilette said.

"Like what?"

"Well . . . I thought you might have some questions."

"About what?"

Gilette fidgeted in his chair.

"I guess you're not gonna make this easy on me, huh, Todd?" the outlaw asked.

"Why should I?" Todd asked. "You didn't make things easy on me and Ma when you left."

"I know," Gilette said, "I'm . . ." He let it trail off just when Clint thought he was going to say "sorry."

"The people in town treated her like shit after you left," Todd said. "She finally died of a broken heart."

"I . . . didn't know."

"Did you think about it at all?" Todd asked. "Did you think about what you did to us?"

"To tell you the truth, Todd, no, I didn't think about it," Gilette said, "I thought about what was ahead of me, not what was behind me."

"Well, that was convenient," Todd said. "You could forget about the wife and son you left behind."

"I had to concentrate on what I was doing, Todd," Gilette said. "That was the lifestyle I picked out. If I didn't concentrate, I could be dead any minute."

"I wish you were dead," Todd said. "I wish you were . . . but I'm glad you're not."

"Why's th—"

"So I can kill you myself," Todd said. He looked at Clint. "Gimme my rifle."

"Not right now, Todd."

"You said you would."

"I said after you talked I would," Clint said. "You and your pa still have some talking to do."

"I'm through talkin'," Todd said. "I came here to kill him and that's what I aim to do."

"I don't blame you for wantin' to kill me, Todd," Gilette said. "But you gotta know I ain't just gonna stand by and let you do it."

"I don't care," Todd said. "I don't care if you or some of your men kill me, as long as I kill you first."

"You're real determined," Gilette said, with more than a little pride.

"Damn right I am!" Todd said. "I promised Ma on her grave that I'd kill you, and that's what I'm gonna do." He stood up so fast he knocked over his chair. He glared at Clint, and then back at his father. "And I ain't gonna let nobody stop me!"

He stormed out of the place, leaving Clint and Gilette as the center of attention for the few other diners present.

"Well," Gilette said, "I thought that went well, don't you?"

"At least," Clint said, "nobody got killed . . . yet."

THIRTY-SIX

Clint asked Gilette where he was going to be and the man just said "around." After that he went to find Todd. He checked the hotel, but the boy wasn't there. He was going to check around town but he got an idea and tried the gun shop. Sure enough, Todd was arguing with the owner.

". . . you gotta have somethin' I can buy!"

"Son, you don't have enough money," the man was saying, patiently.

There was a gun on the counter, an old Walker Colt Todd must have been looking for. Clint came up behind the boy and grabbed his arm before he could grab for the gun and cause trouble.

"Come on, Todd."

"Lemme go!"

"I'm sorry, Mister," the man said, "but he just ain't got enough money to buy a gun."

"That's okay," Clint said. "You did the right thing." Clint tightened his grip on Todd's elbow and steered him to the door. He released him when they got outside and Todd rubbed the spot.

"That hurt."

"I can hurt you a lot worse," Clint said. "What did you think you were doing?"

"Getting a gun to do what I came to do," Todd said. "You lied to me. You told me you'd give me your gun back."

"And I will," Clint said, "but not until after we've talked."

"There ain't nothin' to talk about. I'm gonna kill 'im."

"Todd, you're so damned stubborn."

"Are you sayin' you think what he did was right?"

"No, I'm not saying that," Clint said, "but I am saying that what you plan to do is wrong."

"Why?"

Clint sputtered for a moment and all he could come up with was, "You just don't kill your own father."

"He was never a father to me," Todd said. "I only saw him once in a while when he came home, and then that last day, just before he left. Never again after that, and I never heard from him again. Does that sound like a father to you?"

"Well . . . no . . ."

"Then gimme my rifle back!"

"He's not just going to let you kill him, you know."

"Then help me."

"I'm trying to, son," Clint said, "I'm trying to."

Gilette went to see the sheriff after Clint left to go and look for Todd.

"You want me to what?" Marbury asked.

"Throw the boy in jail."

"Are you saying he *is* your son?"

"Yes, he is."

"And you *want* me to throw him in jail?"

"Just as quick as you can."

"But why?"

"To keep him alive."

"But what do I charge him with?"

"I don't know and I don't care," Gilette said. "Just stick him in a cell."

"For how long?"

"Until I tell you to let him out."

"Gilette—"

"Don't forget who gave you this job, Marbury."

"Trace Atkins did."

He was right. Atkins had given Marbury the job, but only after Gilette talked him into it.

"When Atkins tells me to do this," Marbury said, "then I will."

"Fine," Gilette said, pointing his finger at Marbury, "just fine, but if my son ends up dead I'm gonna hold you responsible."

"Hey," Marbury said, "that's not . . ." But Gilette was already out of the office when he said, ". . . fair."

Clint practically dragged Todd back to the hotel and put him in his room.

"This is all I ask, Todd," he said. "Sit here a while and think about what you want to do. Make damned sure you make the right decision, because it's going to stay with you for the rest of your life."

"Okay," Todd said, "I'll do that. I'll think about it . . . but it ain't gonna make a lick of difference."

"Maybe not," Clint said. "Just think it over."

He closed the door, and took the boy's rifle with him. He thought about leaving it in his own room, but figured the boy would look there. He finally decided to take it with him.

He went down to the lobby and stopped right in the center of it. Where was there to go now? And what was there to do? Todd was either going to decide he did or didn't want to kill his father. There wasn't much to be done until that happened.

He went outside, found a straightbacked wooden chair, pulled it over and sat down on it, laying the rifle across his thighs. He'd just sit here and wait for Todd to come to his decision. During that time maybe—just maybe—some solution would present itself to him.

THIRTY-SEVEN

While Clint was seated in front of the hotel Lem and Joe were still camped outside of town, Joe growing more and more impatient.

"If you go into town now Adams will recognize you," Lem said.

"So? It could just be a coincidence."

"I don't think he'd see it that way, Joe," Lem said. "My advice is—"

"I'm tired of your advice."

They both stopped short when they heard horses approaching. In seconds three riders were entering their camp. It was all three of the men they had sent messages to for help. All three were looking for the enhancement their reputations would receive from killing the Gunsmith.

"Well," Joe said, straightening from his squat by the campfire, "it's damn well about time. Now we can get this show on the road."

Lem stood up as well, and said, "The least we can do is let them rest up some. We'll go in tomorrow."

"For sure?" Joe asked.

"Yeah," Lem said, "for sure."

"Okay then," Joe said. "I can wait a little longer as long as I know there's an end in sight."

Both men went to greet their three colleagues.

Clint watched as Eddie Gilette walked across the street and approached him. There was a second chair, and Gilette sat in it.

"He's quite a kid," the outlaw said.

"Yes, he is," Clint agreed.

"You got to get him out of here, Adams," Gilette said. "If he comes after me I may not be able to stop the others—"

"He's your son, Gilette," Clint said. "You better be able to stop them. You better talk to Atkins and enlist his help."

"But if you take him away—"

"I'd have to hogtie him to do it," Clint said, "and I've got too much respect for him to do that to him."

"What good is respect gonna be if he's dead?" Gilette asked.

"That's a question you're going to have to ask your son," Clint replied. "He's the only one who can answer that."

"So, in other words, you're not gonna help me."

Clint turned his head to look right at Gilette.

"Let's get something straight, Gilette," he said. "I'm here to help Todd, not to help you."

"What if I need your help to keep Todd alive?"

"I've already decided to do whatever I have to to keep that boy alive," Clint said. "You can count on that."

"That's all I ask," Gilette said, and he stood up. "I'll go and talk to Atkins and be back tomorrow."

"Okay."

The outlaw stepped down from the boardwalk, then turned back.

"See if you can keep the kid from wandering around," he said. "He'll never find the canyon on his own."

"I think I can do that," Clint said.

"What about you?"

"What about me?" Clint asked.

"You interested in seeing Dead Horse Canyon."

"As far as I'm concerned," Clint said, "Dead Horse Canyon is still a myth. No, I'm not interested at all. Not as long as you come back here tomorrow so that we don't have to go looking for you to finish this."

"I'll be back tomorrow," Gilette said. "Count on it."

"I will."

Gilette nodded, turned and walked away.

Once the outlaw was out of sight Clint waited until the man had mounted up and ridden out of town again. Then he got up himself and went inside to tell Todd what was happening.

Gilette couldn't believe how Todd looked, or how stubborn he was. He got his look from Gilette, but that stubborn streak, that came from his mother, for sure.

Gilette wasn't sure what he was going to tell Atkins about Todd. Hell, he wasn't even sure what he was going to tell him about Adams, and that had been the reason he'd gone to town in the first place. All he had to do was keep anyone else from going into town, looking for trouble.

He was surprised at how protective he felt toward a son he hardly even knew.

"He'll be back," Clint said.

"How do you know?"

"He said he would."

"And you believe him?"

"I do."

"Why?"

"Because he wants to finish this as badly as you do."

"I don't think he wants to finish it as bad as I do," Todd said. "And I know he don't want to finish it the *way* I do."

"Well," Clint said, "one way or another it'll be finished tomorrow."

"That suits me fine," Todd said. "Just fine."

THIRTY-EIGHT

When Gilette got back to Dead Horse Canyon it didn't
feel the same as it usually did. Was this life wearing thin
on him? Was he ready to leave it, just as Atkins seemed
to be?

As he rode in Trace Atkins came out of his cabin and
waited. Gilette dismounted, handed his horse off to someone and walked over to Atkins.

"Let's talk inside," the outlaw leader said. He turned
and entered the cabin, and Gilette followed. Belinda was
not around.

"Eddie," Atkins said, turning to face Gilette, "I'm
leavin'."

"Well, that's no surprise."

"You knew?"

"Of course I knew, Trace," Gilette said. "It's obvious
what's goin' on between you and Belinda."

"What about the others?" Atkins asked. "Do they
know?"

"Probably not."

"You'll have to take over."

"I'm not sure I'll be here, either."

"What?" That shocked Atkins. "You're always here.

You're the one thing about this valley that never changes."

"Everything changes eventually."

"Well, if I leave and you leave . . . give the gang back to Starling, for all I care," Atkins said.

"Starling's past it, Trace," Gilette said.

"Then who?"

"What do you care?" Gilette asked. "Take Belinda and go. Things will sort themselves out here. Maybe Tayback will take over."

"Tayback?"

"I said maybe . . ."

"What's goin' on, Eddie?" Atkins asked. "What happened in town? Is Adams really there?"

"He's there, all right."

"And the boy?"

Gilette nodded. "He's mine."

"That must have been a shock."

"It was," Gilette said. "He's the spitting image of me."

"Why's he here? To join up?"

"His mother died," Gilette said, "and he wants to kill me. It's a promise he made on her grave."

"What are you gonna do?"

"Keep him away from here," Gilette said, "and the only way I can think to do that is to leave. I don't want any of the boys doin' anything to 'protect' me, you know?"

"They'd kill him in a heartbeat."

"I know it."

"So . . . should we tell them together? That we're both leavin'?"

"Make an announcement, you mean?" Gilette asked. "Naw. Why not just pack and leave?"

"We got to tell them something."

"Let's bring in Tayback, then, and a few of the others. They can pass the word along."

"Who looks like a likely leader?" Atkins asked. "You always seem to know that ahead of time."

"You remember that?" Gilette asked. "I didn't think you did."

"I remember that you pushed me to take over from Starling," Atkins said. "You been pushing anyone to take over from me?"

"Not lately. When were you planning to leave?"

"Belinda's in a hurry," Atkins said. "I thought in the morning. She's tellin' the other girls."

"That'll get the word out fast enough," Gilette said. "I guess I'll leave in the morning, too."

"What are you gonna do?"

"Don't know, yet," Gilette said. "Try to convince my son not to become a killer, I guess."

"Apologize to him?"

Gilette shook his head.

"I don't think that would do any good."

"You might try it and see," Atkins said. "I know I wouldn't have minded if my old man apologized to me."

"For leavin'?"

"Hell, no," Atkins said. "I wish the sonofabitch did leave. He was always around, and always beatin' on me and my ma. What a stupid bitch she was, staying around to get thumped all the time. Come to think of it, I wouldn't have mind if she apologized, too, for not takin' us away from him."

Gilette seemed to consider the option for a moment, then shook his head and said, "No, it wouldn't do any good."

"Well, it's up to you. You want to bring Tayback and some of the others in here now?"

"Might as well," Gilette said. "They won't have much time to get used to it, as it is."

Gilette started for the door.

"Hey, Eddie."

"What?" Gilette asked, at the door.

"Thanks."

"For what?"

"For seein' somethin' in me that I never saw for myself," Atkins said.

"Sounds like Belinda might be doin' the same thing, Trace."

"I know it," Atkins said. "Anyway, thanks."

"Don't mention it," Gilette said, and went outside.

The three men who rode into Lem and Joe's camp were named Leo, Pete and Johnny. Their last names were of little consequence because they were all the same type. Tied down guns, well worn trail clothes, nondescript faces. Their names would mean nothing to anyone—until they killed the Gunsmith.

"The three of us should ride into town tonight," Johnny said. "Hell, Adams doesn't know what we look like."

"And we can get the lay of the land," Pete said.

"And check out the local law," Leo added.

"According to Tayback," Lem said, "the local law was put there by the Atkins gang, so he's probably not gonna be a problem . . . but this does sound like a good idea. You boys'll be in place when we ride in tomorrow morning."

"I like this idea," Joe said. "At least we'll be gettin' somethin' done today."

They were gathered around the fire, all drinking coffee, and it was Johnny who dumped his remnants into the fire first and stood up.

"Let's get a move on, then," he said to the others. "We want to ride in before dark."

More coffee remnants went into the fire, and the three men mounted up.

THIRTY-NINE

Todd stayed in his room the rest of the evening, and he and Clint did not speak again. Clint assumed that Todd was not coming out until the next day, when Gilette returned. He went to the café to eat alone, then had a tray brought up to Todd's room so the boy wouldn't starve. He then went to the saloon for a beer, forgetting that Doc Page would be hosting his regular game. Luckily, tonight all the seats were occupied and there was no room for Clint, anyway.

The saloon was about half full, which was the reason the three men sitting at a corner table nursing beers stood out. Clint could see them in the mirror behind the bar, and they were very interested in him. This was not an odd occurrence, however, as he was often the object of attention. If they recognized him they were now discussing which of them should try him out and see if he's really the legend he was made out to be. Two things were likely to happen. One of them would get brave and the other two would back him up, or they would each order another beer and forget about it.

Clint was getting ready to leave when he saw Doc Page stand up, don his jacket, and come over to the bar.

He noticed that the physician was wearing a gun and
holster. The night before if he'd been wearing a gun it
would have had to be a sleeve gun.

"Quitting early, Doc?" Clint asked.

"Just thought you ought to know," Doc said, "you're
the subject of some attention."

"Three men, corner table," Clint said. "I noticed."

"Thought you might," Doc said. "No harm double-
checking, though."

"I appreciate the thought."

"Buy you another one?" Page asked, noticing that
Clint was almost done with his beer.

Clint looked over at the poker table, where the five
players were looking over toward he and Doc.

"Don't worry," Doc Page said, "the game can survive
without me for a while."

"Well, sure," Clint said, even though he'd been planning to turn in after he finished the beer he had. "I'll
have another one."

Doc waved at the bartender, who brought over two
beers.

"Did you get done what you came here to get done?"
Page asked.

"Not yet," Clint said. "Probably tomorrow. Tell me
something, Doc."

"What's that?"

"How'd you end up here?" Clint asked. "Seems to me
a man like you would enjoy . . . a broader scope for his
talents."

"Talents?"

"Poker," Clint said, "medicine."

"Neither of those are talents," Doc said. "One's a vice,
the other a trap."

"A trap?" Clint asked. "I assume we're talking about
medicine?"

"I didn't come here to practice medicine," Doc said. "I came here to get away from . . . things. Instead, I find a town that has no doctor, but has a lot of people either getting sick, shot or pregnant. What was I to do? I couldn't ignore them, so I ended up practicing medicine."

"What was it, exactly, you were trying to get away from?"

Doc took a sidelong look at the three men who were still sort of sizing Clint up and said, "That sort of thing. I was on my way to having a reputation something like yours—well, not as big as yours, probably, but you know what I mean."

And so it became obvious that Doc had recognized Clint for who he was, but had not mentioned it at the poker table.

"I do."

"I decided to get out before it happened."

"How long have you been here?"

"Fifteen years."

Clint whistled soundlessly.

"Fifteen years in one place," he said, shaking his head. "I think that would kill me."

"Well, I think it's kept me alive," Doc said. "See this gun I'm wearin'?"

"I see it." It was an old gun, but it was clean and well cared for.

"This is the first time I'm wearing it since I came here."

"And what's the occasion?"

"You're here."

Suddenly, Clint looked wary.

"Doc—"

"I'm not lookin' to try you, so don't worry about that," Doc said, "but somebody will. Before you leave, somebody—maybe those three—will have to try you, and I'll be there to back you up."

"Well, I appreciate that, Doc, but why?"

"To make sure that none of my people—see, these have become my people now—end up getting hurt. So you see, I'm not so much backing you as I am protecting them."

"Isn't that what the sheriff's for?"

"The sheriff is worthless," Doc said. "He works for the Atkins gang, and he won't be any help to you."

"Tell me something else, Doc," Clint said. "Have you ever been to Dead Horse Canyon?"

"Once," Doc said. "Trace Atkins took a bullet and I had to dig it out."

"So you've actually been there?"

"Yes."

"Did they blindfold you?"

"No."

"Why not?"

"Because," Doc said, "I promised I wouldn't give up the location."

"And I'll bet that's a promise you intend to keep."

"Yes, sir."

"Then I won't ask anymore about it."

"Good."

Clint put the second beer down half full and said, "Well, thanks for the beer, Doc, and the backup—if I need it."

"Oh, you'll need it."

"And you haven't forgot how to use that?" Clint asked, looking at the man's gun.

"You of all people," Doc Page said, "should know that's not something a man forgets."

FORTY

Clint was a bit surprised that he got out of the saloon without an incident. The three men had put away quite a few beers while he was there and he was sure they were going to build up some false courage between them. Instead, he left the saloon and made it to his hotel without any altercations.

The three men—Johnny, Pete and Leo—were, in fact, building some false courage on beer, and discussing the possibility of taking on the Gunsmith without Lem and Joe.

"First of all," Johnny said, "that Joe's no gunhand."

"We can count on Lem for help, though," Leo said.

"So that would give us one more gun," Pete said. "Do we really need one more gun for us to be able to take care of any one man?"

They all agreed that they did not. However, a cooler head—Johnny's—did prevail in the end.

"Wai', wai', wai' a minute," he said, waving his hand. "Tomorrow we'll have five guns, and daylight, and not so much beer in us. I vote we wait for tomorrow."

Leo and Pete looked at each other, but did not answer.

"If we wait until tomorrow," Johnny added, "we can have another beer now."

"Okay!" Pete said.

"We wait!" Leo said, and they all had another beer.

Clint paused by Todd's door to listen in. He didn't hear anything so he turned the doorknob slowly and opened the door a crack. The lamp was still lit and Todd had fallen asleep on the bed, fully dressed. Clint really wasn't afraid that the boy might have left the hotel to look for the canyon in the dark. He was young, but he wasn't stupid and, besides, Clint still had his rifle.

He closed the door and went to his own room for some shuteye.

Eddie Gilette looked around his cabin and realized that he would not miss it. He had lived in this cabin, off and on, for about a dozen years or so, and it had not changed at all. A few days ago he would have said that he hadn't changed, either, but now he knew that he had.

Still looking around the cabin he knew there was nothing there he wanted to take with him. When he left he'd be taking a horse, and his guns, and that was it. That was all he had to show for all the years riding the outlaw trail, after all the money he'd stolen from banks and stages and trains.

Tayback and the others hadn't been happy when he and Atkins told them they were both leaving. It had taken some talking to calm them down. He'd even had to step between Tayback and Atkins when Tayback accused the outlaw leader of being afraid of the Gunsmith.

"I'll go to town right now and blow his head off myself," Tayback said.

"Do it!" Atkins had replied. "Without a doubt, that

would make you the new leader of this gang. Go ahead and do it!"

Tayback hesitated just long enough for everyone to know that when he said, "I just might," he really had no intention of trying it. He had turned at the point and stormed out, and the other men had followed.

By now it was probably all over camp that he and Atkins were leaving, but he didn't care. His mind was made up.

He was out of here.

Atkins and Belinda lay together in his bed. He was asleep, and she was lying with her head on his chest, listening to his breathing, too excited to sleep because he had finally agreed that they would leave Dead Horse Canyon the next day.

It was only because she was awake that she heard the door creak open.

By midnight Will Tayback had most of the men in the gang worked up over the fact that both Atkins and Gilette were leaving at the same time.

"We're supposed to be a family," Tayback said. "Share everything. Share the women. Well, we ain't been sharing Belinda, have we?"

The other men shook their heads.

"And we ain't never shared those cabins they both live in."

"Leader and second always get the cabins, Will," a man named Birmingham said.

"And who made those rules?" Tayback demanded.

"Gilette?" someone said.

"That's right. Now they're breaking the rules. Atkins is taking Belinda, and who knows what else the two of them are taking. We were never in on counting the take;

it was always the two of them. Who knows how much money they hid away between them?"

"We sure don't," someone said.

"That's right."

"So what do we do, Will?"

Tayback stood up, and in that moment he assumed command of the entire gang—except for Starling, who was watching the proceeding with a wary eye. He thought he knew what was coming, and he didn't want any part of it.

Quietly, he slipped away and headed for Gilette's cabin to warn him.

"I'll tell you what we're gonna do," Tayback said. "We're gonna show them that nobody leaves this gang except in a box!"

The others agreed.

"And nobody takes rightfully what belongs to all of us."

"Right again!" somebody yelled.

Tayback drew his gun.

"Now, I know I could be the new leader just by waiting and lettin' them ride out tomorrow," he said, and was rewarded by mostly nodding heads, "but that ain't the way you take over a gang like this, is it?"

"No!" a few men said.

"No," Tayback said, "it ain't." He lifted his gun over his head and said, "This is!"

In reply some men simply shouted yeah, while others took out their own guns.

"Come on!" Tayback said.

Starling knocked on Gilette's door, then pounded on it until Gilette finally opened it. He was bleary-eyed as if he'd been asleep, or almost asleep.

"Wha—what is it? Starling, is that you?"

Starling pushed Gilette back into his cabin, stepped in after him and slammed the door.

"Do you hear what's goin' on out there?"

"I heard somethin'," Gilette said, "but I got to get an early start in the morning, Starling."

"Eddie," Starling said, "you ain't gettin' out of here unless you leave tonight."

"Whataya mean?"

"Tayback's got them all worked up," Starling said. "They're gonna take over."

"What's to take over?" Gilette asked. "After Atkins and I leave they can have the whole place."

"They don't want it tomorrow," Starling said, "they want it tonight. And they don't want it left for them, they wanna take it!"

"Are you sure you're not givin' Tayback too much cred—"

That was when they heard the shots, and Gilette turned and ran to get his gun off the bedpost.

And then the door was kicked in!

FORTY-ONE

The next morning Lem and Joe rode into town just after first light. They rode down main street brazen as you please, because now they didn't care if Clint Adams saw them or not.

And he did. He was looking out the window, having risen and dressed early. He was actually watching for Eddie Gilette, but he recognized Lem and Joe right away.

"Trouble," he told himself.

Lem and Joe rode past the hotel and when they reached the next block the other three men they had aligned themselves with stepped into the street.

"Where is he?" Lem asked.

"He's in the hotel," Johnny said.

"You guys look awful," Joe said.

"Hung over," Lem said, "that's what they look."

"We'll do our part," Leo said, with a scowl.

"We saw him last night, in the saloon," Pete said. "Clint Adams. We saw him."

"You didn't try anything, did you?" Lem asked.

"Why would we do that, Lem?" Leo asked. "We're here to help you, remember?"

"Just as long as you remember."

Lem and Joe dismounted and tied their horses off.

"Hey, look," Leo said.

They all turned and looked in the direction of the hotel and saw Clint Adams standing outside.

"He knows we're here," Joe said.

"Good," Lem said. "Then we won't have to go looking for him."

"Hey," Pete asked, "after we do this can we get into Dead Horse Canyon?"

Lem didn't know the answer to that, but he said, "We'll see. Right now, let's take care of business."

Clint stepped out of the hotel and saw the five men standing together. Lem and Joe and the three from the saloon the night before. He knew they were trouble when he first saw them.

Clint contemplated going upstairs and waking Todd to tell him to stay in his room, but if he was asleep then he was in his room, so what was the point? Better that the boy would wake up and find that it was all over with. Then all he'd have to deal with was his father.

Five against one. Pretty bad odds, and there didn't seem much chance that he'd be able to talk them out of it this time. Lem and Joe had help, and that was all they needed to build the courage they'd lacked in Broken Branch.

Clint stepped down into the street.

"Look at him," Pete said. "You gotta admire the guy. He's gonna face the five of us by himself."

"Probably kill some of us, too," Leo said.

The five men exchanged glances, wondering who'd be dead when this was all over.

"Hell," Johnny said, "we all gotta die sometime."

"Good point, John," Lem said. "Come on, let's walk."

The five men fanned out in the street and started walking toward Clint Adams.

This was not going to be one of the smartest things he'd ever done, Clint thought. He hated the idea of the last thing he ever did being something not very smart, because when you were dead people only remembered the last thing you did. Like Hickok. Everybody remembered that he was shot in the back while playing poker. Hell, the goddamned hand he'd been holding had become more famous than him.

Clint reached behind him to touch the Colt New Line he'd tucked into his belt there before coming down. It had been in his saddlebags, and was the weapon he usually used as a hideout gun. He was going to have to get real close to use it, but it was comforting to have a second gun when you were going up against five men.

The five men saw him before Clint did.

"Who the hell is that?" Lem asked.

They all stared at the man dressed in black who had stepped out of an alley and was now approaching Clint Adams.

"Hey," Johnny said, "we saw him last night, too, in the saloon."

"Doin' what?" Lem asked.

"Playin' poker," Leo said.

"And talkin' to Adams," Pete added. "In fact, he bought him a beer."

"Who is he?" Joe asked.

"We only heard folks callin' him Doc," Leo said.

"Page," Johnny said, "they called him Doc Page."

"Is he a doctor?" Lem asked. "Or a gunfighter?"

"Right now," Johnny said, "he sort of looks like both . . . don't he?"

Clint heard the approach of a man to his right and turned his head. He saw Doc Page crossing the street toward him.

"Doc."

"I told you I'd back you," Page said. "I thought it would be against three men, though."

"Don't feel obligated, Doc," Clint said. "I won't hold you to it."

"It's still my town."

"There's nobody on the street," Clint said, "nobody to get hurt by a stray bullet. Go back to your office, Doc. No hard feelings."

"Ah," Doc Page said, "I got nothin' better to do, anyway."

He stopped about three feet from Clint, and turned to face the approaching five men.

"What do we know about these characters?" Doc asked.

"The two on the left, I talked them down once before."

"Looks like they came back with help."

"Looks like."

"Ain't gonna talk them out of it this time?"

"I doubt it."

"Too bad," Doc said, and then added, "for them."

FORTY-TWO

Clint had no idea how good Doc Page was with a gun, but the man certainly appeared to be confident.

"Split them up?" Page asked.

"You take the two on the right," Clint said, "I'll take my old friends on the left. How's that?"

"That's okay," Doc said, "but who gets the jasper in the middle?"

"Up for grabs," Clint said.

"Suits me."

"Doc?"

"Yeah?"

"When did you say was the last time you fired your gun?"

"I didn't say."

"Why not?"

"You don't want to know."

"Oh."

"Two against five," Lem said, "that's still good odds."

Johnny, Pete and Leo were thinking, Two against *four*, because none of them had any confidence in Joe with a gun.

Which made the odds two to one.

"Look," Lem said, sensing some doubt building, "we don't know who this other fella is. He may be no help to Adams at all. It's the Gunsmith we still got to concentrate on."

"Okay," Pete said. He was standing all the way to the left. "I'll take the dandy in the suit. The rest of you go for Adams."

"Sounds like a plan," Lem said.

When they got close enough Clint saw it. He saw it in their eyes, and in their body language. Four of them were concentrating on him. He also saw that one of the men from Broken Branch—Joe, he remembered—looked real nervous and skittish.

"Clint—"

"I see it," Clint said.

They seemed to be thinking alike, which Clint found comforting.

This might actually work.

Todd woke to the shots, a barrage of them coming from outside. He ran to his window and looked out. There were seven men in the street. Four were lying face up or down, one was on his knees, Clint and another man were standing with their guns drawn.

He turned and ran from the room.

Clint had fired two quick shots, taking Lem and the man to his immediate left in the chest. Doc fired three shots, because his first had been low, and to the left, taking the end man in the hip. His second shot finished him, and he still had time to kill the other man who was his responsibility.

Clint changed his targets when he realized that Joe was

going to be no help to his friends. As soon as the shooting started he fell to his knees and raised his hands into the air.

And now it was quiet.

"Doc?"

"I'm not hit. You?"

"Fine."

"What about him?" Doc asked, indicating the man on his knees.

"I don't think he's going to be any trouble."

Clint walked over to Joe, took his gun from his holster and tossed it away. Doc went over to the other four men to check and see if they were dead.

"They're all done for," he announced.

"Don't kill me," Joe was saying. "Don't kill me."

"You're not worth a bullet," Clint said. He put his foot on the man's chest and pushed. Joe went down onto his back and stayed there, his hands covering his face.

"Clint!"

He turned to see Todd running at him. The boy seemed about to throw his arms around him, but brought himself up short.

"Are you all right?" he asked.

"I'm fine," Clint said, "thanks to Doc, here. He backed me up."

"Is—is one of them my pa?"

"No, Todd," Clint said, "your pa isn't here, yet. This was those two from Broken Branch and some friends of theirs."

"What's goin' on?"

Clint turned and saw the sheriff approaching.

"Nice of you to show up, Sheriff," Clint said, "after it's all over."

"Now look, Adams—"

"We've got one for your jail," Clint said, "and four for the undertaker."

"Clint," Doc Page said, "rider comin' in."

"Maybe it's my pa," Todd said. "Gimme my rifle!"

"It's not your pa, Todd," Clint said.

They all watched as the rider approached and when he got close enough they could see that he was injured.

"Doc?" Clint said. "Know him?"

"It's Starling," Doc said. "From the canyon."

The man reached them but before he could say a word he fell from the saddle. Both Clint and Doc leaped forward and caught him.

"He's been shot," Doc said. "Let's get him to my office."

"Todd," Clint said, "collect all the guns from the street and take them to the sheriff's office, then join us at the Doc's."

"Right."

"Let's go, Doc," Clint said, and between them they carried the injured man to the doctor's office.

FORTY-THREE

Clint and Todd waited in Doc's office while he worked on Starling in his surgery.

"I don't think he's comin'," Todd said.

"Maybe not."

"I'll have to go and find him."

Clint said nothing.

"Are you gonna gimme my rifle?"

"Didn't you see enough killing today, Todd?"

"I didn't see my pa dead," Todd said. "That's when it'll be enough for me. Not before."

Before Clint could reply the door opened and Doc stepped into the room.

"How is he, Doc?"

"I don't think he'll make it," Doc said. "He's got two bullets in him, and I think one hit a lung. I'm surprised he got this far."

"What's he got to say?" Clint asked. "Anything?"

"Yeah," Doc said, "he keeps saying' 'it's all over.' He says it again and again."

"What's he mean?"

"I don't know."

"And you say he came from the canyon?" Clint asked.

"Starling was the gang's leader before Trace Atkins took over," Doc said.

"And he stayed?"

"He had no place else to go," Doc said. "Starling *never* leaves Dead Horse Canyon. I don't understand it."

"Something really bad must have happened out there," Clint said, giving Doc a long look.

Doc sighed and said, "All right. I'll take you out there—but I might be putting my life . . . and all our lives . . . in danger . . ."

"Doc," Clint said, "I think something is seriously wrong out there. Somebody's got to take a look."

"I know," Doc said. He looked at Todd. "The boy, too?"

Clint saw Todd looking at him and said, "Yes, the boy, too."

"All right," Doc said. "Let me get cleaned up and get somebody to watch Starling, and then I'll lead you out there."

Doc went back into the surgery and Clint looked at Todd.

"Well, Todd, it looks like you're going to get your wish," he said. "We're going to Dead Horse Canyon."

"That's half my wish, anyway," Todd said.

"That's funny," Doc said.

"What is?" Clint asked.

"There's usually a guard right here."

"Are we there?" Todd asked.

"We're close," Doc said. "You usually have to go through a bunch of checkpoints."

"Let's keep going," Clint said. Even under the present circumstances he was pleased with the way his new horse, Eclipse, was handling the rocky footing. Doc and

Todd both had experienced Western mounts who were having no trouble at all.

They passed the second and third checkpoints without being stopped.

And then, suddenly, they were in.

"This is it," Doc said. "This is Dead Horse Canyon."

The sides of the canyon were steep, and this was the only way in or out.

"Where's the camp?" Clint asked.

"Further in."

They rode for a few minutes more and then found the first body. A man was lying on the ground, face down. Doc dismounted and checked him.

"He's dead," he announced. "Shot."

"Know him?" Clint asked.

"Just by his face," Doc said, mounting up again.

They rode on, came to a second and a third body, obviously dead of gunshot wounds. Clearly, Clint had been right. Something terrible had happened.

And then they saw the camp. Clint saw three cabins, some campfires, and bodies. There were five or six men standing around, or sitting, some holding their heads, or other injuries. As they rode up to them he saw that there were eight or nine of them, but nine of them were paying no attention to them. Some of them were saddling horses, or tying bedrolls to their saddles.

Finally, one man looked up at them as they approached.

"What happened here, Seth?" Doc asked.

"It's bad, Doc," Seth said. "It's all over."

"Are you okay?" Seth's hand was bandaged.

Seth held up his hand and looked at it.

"It's okay," Seth said. "I'm one of the lucky ones. They went crazy, Doc. Plumb crazy."

"What happened here?"

"Tayback," Seth said, "he went nuts. See, Atkins and Gilette, they was leavin' today. They'd had enough of this life. Atkins was takin' one of the women, Belinda, with him. Tayback didn't like that. He said it was against the rules—and it was. He also said they had some money hidden."

"And what happened?" Clint asked.

"Tayback and a bunch them, they went to Atkins's cabin, kicked in the door and . . . and then the shootin' started. Once Atkins was dead, Tayback claimed to be the leader. But then it got crazy. Somebody back shot Tayback and said *they* were the leader, and then everybody was shooting. God . . . it went on most of the night, and at first light those of us who were left . . . well, we kinda came to our senses. We realized it was all over. Dead Horse Canyon was . . . well, dead. We're leavin', Doc. Splittin' up and leavin'." Seth mounted up and said, "I gotta go. Might be some of them here needs doctorin', though."

"I'll check it out, Seth," Doc said. "Good luck to you."

"Where's Gilette?" Clint asked Seth.

"That second cabin is his," Seth said. "Have a look."

Doc dismounted, walked over to a man who was holding his side, then to another who was bleeding from the head.

"I've got to help them," Doc said to Clint.

"That's okay, Doc," Clint said. He turned to Todd. "You're in Dead Horse Canyon, son. What do you want to do?"

"Let's have a look at that second cabin," Todd said.

They rode over and dismounted in front of it. Todd took his rifle, which Clint had returned to him. He walked to the door with Clint behind him, and then stopped.

"Well?" Clint asked. "This is what you wanted."

Todd took a deep breath. The door was hanging on

one hinge, having already been kicked in. He pushed it open and stepped inside.

On the floor, between the bed and the table, was Eddie Gilette. Apparently, he'd made a run for his gun and got it, but then a barrage of bullets had brought him down. From the way he looked Clint figured he'd been hit twelve, maybe fifteen times.

"They shot him to pieces," Clint said, "because he wanted to leave the gang."

Todd stared down at his father, his face slack.

"Why?" he asked, his voice barely audible. "Why did he want to leave?"

"Maybe," Clint said, "it was because of you."

Todd looked at Clint, then back down at his dead father. Suddenly, and viciously, he drew back his leg and kicked the dead body, hard. Just once.

"You sonofabitch!" he shouted. "You were too late! Too damn late!"

Todd dropped his rifle, turned, pressed his face into Clint's chest and began to sob uncontrollably. Clint put both his arms around the boy to console him.

"It'll be all right now, Todd," he said. "It'll be all right."